Red Lips & White Lies

Captivating

USA TODAY BESTSELLING AUTHOR
BELLA MATTHEWS

CAPTIVATING

A KROYDON HILLS LEGACY NOVEL

RED LIPS & WHITE LIES
BOOK FOUR

BELLA MATTHEWS

Editor: Dena Mastrogiovanni, Red Pen Editing

Cover Designer: Val, Books And Moods

Interior Formatting: Brianna Cooper

SENSITIVE CONTENT

This book contains sensitive content that could be triggering.
Please see my website for a full list.

WWW.AUTHORBELLAMATTHEWS.COM

This book is dedicated to all the women who grew up with a crazy group of guys as your best friends. We are a different breed.
XOXO Bella

When all else fails, roll the windows down, turn the radio up, and sing at the top of your lungs.

— BELLA'S SECRET THOUGHTS

CAST OF CHARACTERS

The Kings Of Kroydon Hills Family

- **Declan & Annabelle Sinclair**
  - Everly Sinclair - 28
  - Grace Sinclair - 28
  - Nixon Sinclair - 27
  - Leo Sinclair - 26
  - Hendrix Sinclair - 23

- **Brady & Nattie Ryan**
  - Noah Ryan - 25
  - Lilah Ryan - 25
  - Dillan Ryan - 22
  - Asher Ryan - 16

- **Aiden & Sabrina Murphy**
  - Jameson Murphy - 25
  - Finn Murphy - 22

- **Bash & Lenny Beneventi**
  - Maverick Beneventi - 25
  - Ryker Beneventi - 23

- **Cooper & Carys Sinclair**
  - Lincoln Sinclair - 18
  - Lochlan Sinclair - 18
  - Lexie Sinclair - 18

- **Coach Joe & Katherine Sinclair**
  - Callen Sinclair - 28

The Kingston Family

- **Ashlyn & Brandon Dixon**
    - Madeline Kingston - 29
    - Raven Dixon - 13

- **Max & Daphne Kingston**
    - Serena Kingston - 22

- **Scarlet & Cade St. James**
    - Brynlee St. James - 28
    - Killian St. James - 26
    - Olivia St. James - 24

- **Becket & Juliette Kingston**
    - Easton Hayes - 33
    - Kenzie Hayes - 27
    - Blaise Kingston - 17

- **Sawyer & Wren Kingston**
    - Knox Kingston - 21
    - Crew Kingston - 18

- **Hudson & Maddie Kingston**
    - Teagan Kingston - 22
    - Aurora Kingston - 19
    - Brooklyn Kingston - 14

- **Amelia & Sam Beneventi**
    - Maddox Beneventi - 27
    - Caitlin Beneventi - 24
    - Roman Beneventi - 22

- ○ Lucky Beneventi - 20

- **Lenny & Bash Beneventi**
  - ○ Maverick Beneventi - 25
  - ○ Ryker Beneventi - 23

- **Jace & India Kingston**
  - ○ Cohen Kingston - 21
  - ○ Saylor Kingston - 20
  - ○ Atlas Kingston - 13
  - ○ Asher Kingston - 13

For family trees, please visit my website
www.authorbellamatthews.com

Not so patiently waiting for the IDGAF chapter of my life.
Anytime now, buddy. Any. Time.

—*Lilah's Secret Thoughts*

Pop princess who got rich writing love songs doesn't know what love is.

Hey everyone, and welcome back to *Just the Tip*, everyone's favorite column, where we gather your most beloved celebrities to talk tips and tricks of their trade. How they made it. What they wish they knew then that they know now, and would they do it all again, given the chance.

We recently had a chance to sit down with America's sweetheart, pop princess Lilah Ryan, and her twin brother and band leader, Noah Ryan, where they discuss love, loss, touring, and everything in between.

Q: Well, Lilah, I feel like I wouldn't be doing my job if I didn't start with everyone's favorite question to ask you.

Lilah looks down at her lap before raising her face and giving us a dazzling smile.

Lilah: Bring it on, Jenny.

Q: You're known for your love songs as much as for your breakup anthems. But you're awfully tight-lipped when it comes to your personal life. Your fans are dying to know— are you currently seeing anyone?

Lilah: Not currently, no.

Q: Come on. There's no one special?

Lilah: Define special.

Lilah's coy smile is in full effect as she leans back in her chair, legs crossed and hands tucked primly in her lap.

Q: Someone who's inspired a song or two, maybe?

Lilah: (Laughing) No. Not right now.

Q: Has there ever been? I mean, with songs like "Swear On My Heart," and "So Pretty When You Lie," you have to have had a great love, right? The kind that changes everything?

Lilah: I thought maybe there was once. *(Pauses for a moment as she chooses her words as carefully as she writes her lyrics.)* But I was wrong.

2

*N*oah grabs my iPad out of my hands and closes the cover. "What are you reading that shit for, anyway?"

"Because I want to know how they managed to twist our words. You know they always do." I roll my eyes and look at the stars in the black sky as they fly by. Another night, another highway. At least this one leads home. "It's not even good writing. Seriously." With frustration building, I reach for the iPad, but Noah tosses it in his duffle bag, and he wraps an arm around my shoulders.

"Ignore it, Tink. They're grasping at straws because you didn't give them what they wanted. We'll be home in twenty minutes." He tips his head back against the seat and stretches his long legs in front of him. "Try to relax."

I lean my head on his shoulder as our phones chime in sync.

That can only mean one thing . . .

I look up at my brother and roll my eyes. "Did you tell her we were coming home today?"

"Nope. But I told Dad, and you know she checks the app."

"Same thing," I murmur as I pull my phone from my pocket and open the text chat we have with our parents and our sister and brother.

MOM

Life360 says you're on your way into Kroydon Hills. Are you coming here?

DAD

Give them a minute to breathe, Natalie. It's late.

MOM

Brady Ryan . . . if you like lying in this bed next to me and not on the couch downstairs, you will hush.

DILLAN

OMG, Mom. Chill. You'll see them tomorrow.

MOM

Why is everyone ganging up on me?

ASHER

I'm on the side of it's late, and I'm trying to sleep. If you guys come tonight, try not to wake me up.

DILLAN

Sleep? It's not that late. Has your girlfriend even scurried down Mom's trellis yet?

ASHER

Don't be a brat, Dillan. She went out the front door. And at least I'm not twenty-two and still living at home.

DILLAN

Whatever you say, oopsie baby.

MOM

Dillan . . . be nice to your brother. His girlfriend doesn't climb in and out of his window.

DAD

. . .

"Jesus Christ. One of us needs to put them out of their misery before Asher tells Mom he lost his virginity last year and she strokes out before we get home." Noah tries to take my phone from my hand, but I elbow his ribs and move away.

"Get your own phone." I never let anyone, not even Noah, text from my phone. The fucker has gotten me in trouble more than once.

> LILAH
>
> We're still fifteen minutes from town. But the car service is dropping us at our own places tonight. I really just want my own bed.

> MOM
>
> How can you want your own bed when you've never even slept in it, young lady?

> DAD
>
> Sweetheart . . . let her go to her new house. She's excited. We'll see them both tomorrow. Right, kids?

I look over at Noah and laugh. "Remind me why we let her have Life360, please . . ."

Noah shrugs and smiles. "It's not like it's a new thing. Mom's always been a little nuts."

> NOAH
>
> How about we come for breakfast tomorrow?

> LILAH
>
> Brunch. I want to sleep in.

> MOM
>
> Fine. But make sure you bring your bodyguard with you. One is waiting for you at your house.

> LILAH
>
> Mother!

"What the fuck—" I snap my head to Noah and instantly see red. "You knew."

It's not a question because the answer is written all over his guilty face.

"I sure did, and I agreed with them." He's completely unapologetic, and I suddenly have the urge to stop the car and walk home. That or maybe junk-punch him. "I know you feel safe here, Lilah, but we still have to be careful. We don't know who set the fucking bombs. If they hadn't found them in the security sweep, they could have taken out us and thousands of people. I don't give a shit if you're pissed. You're alive, and you're going to stay that way. The label expanded your security. Guess you're going to test out that guest house sooner than you thought."

"Fine. But they don't come inside." I refuse to look at Noah or my phone. I've spent the last year working with designers on every last detail for my brand-new house, and the thought of sleeping there tonight has been what's gotten me through these past few weeks of the tour. It's supposed to be my refuge. My haven. With ten acres of privacy and walls of windows in nearly every room, every painstaking detail has been thought-out so I can feel as free as possible while maintaining as much privacy as possible.

I absolutely refuse to let anyone ruin the small speck of normalcy I've earned.

And I've earned it.

I swore after spending two entire years touring, I wasn't going back out right away. But our label had other plans and strong-armed me into what they called a small six-month tour. The last two months were postponed because of the security breach. We're going to discuss rescheduling it in a few days. But until then, I'm going home to my own house, and I'm going to live like a happy hermit.

At least that's what I tell myself until my phone chimes again.

MOM

Fine. I'll have breakfast ready at ten tomorrow. I know everyone can't wait to see you guys.

I look at Noah. "Hell no. I'm not ready to see the whole family. Not yet."

Noah's eyes soften as he shakes his head. "I get it."

LILAH

Just us, Mom.

MOM

But honey . . .

DAD

Just us, Tink. I promise.

When Mom was growing up, everyone called her Tinker Bell. But Dad says the minute I was born, that's what she called me. Her little fairy. Tiny, feisty, and even more blonde than she was. I think she was just happy to give the nickname to someone else.

LILAH

Thanks, Daddy. See you tomorrow.

"Thanks, Daddy," Noah mocks, and I stick my middle finger in the air and close my eyes. "Would now be a bad

time to tell you I'm crashing with you for the next few days too?"

"What?" I give in and punch him the way I've wanted to for the past ten minutes. Not in the junk, but close enough. "Why? What's wrong with the condo?"

"Jamie's crashing there. After they lost their playoff game, he wanted to get the hell out of DC, and we only have one functioning bedroom in the condo right now." At least he has the good graces to look guilty. I get it, and normally I wouldn't care. Jamie has crashed with us for years in his off-season. Our cousin is the best defensive tackle in the NFL. He's also one of my closest friends, but the fucker refuses to buy his own place, and he's messy as shit.

"Fine. But just you," I warn him. "I mean it, Noah."

"I hear ya. Just me . . ."

*A*n hour later, I'm changed and sitting on my brand-new oversized, overstuffed, pale-blue couch that I absolutely love and may never leave. Noah is strumming his favorite acoustic guitar, *Baby*, next to me, while I work on the song I've had stuck in my head for the past few weeks. I can't seem to get it on paper no matter how hard I try.

The melody is there, but the lyrics . . . they're just not.

~~Another city. Another lonely night.~~

Well, that lyric sucks.

I scribble a line through the shitty lyric, trying to figure out exactly when I started to write whiney music. It's never been my vibe, and I'm not sure why it keeps coming out that way now.

According to my mom, I've been writing songs since before I learned to write a sentence. The piano came before that, and the guitar came after. It's always been my way to process the world. My reprieve. But right now, it's my biggest stressor because the words aren't coming like they used to. Nothing sounds right, and with each ugly scratch in my notebook, I worry more and more that I've lost *it*.

That thing that makes my songs special.

That magic that filters through my words.

Like I've lost a piece of myself.

Boom. Boom. Boom.

What the— I drop my pen as the booming knock filters in from the front of the house and scares the hell out of me. My eyes fly to Noah's as he strums his guitar like the big bad wolf doesn't sound like he's trying to knock down our door.

"Open up before your bodyguard finds out who the badder guy really is, Tink."

What the fuck? There are so many things wrong with that sentence.

"Maddox?" I ask, surprised, and Noah nods, still strumming his guitar. Well, at least until the banging starts again.

"Hold your fucking horses, Madman."

"What happened to just us?" Sarcasm drips from my words while his long legs eat up the room as I follow behind. "Did you give him the gate code?"

My brother shakes his head, and I brace for Maddox Beneventi when the door swings open, but my breath gets caught in my throat because Maddox isn't alone.

"Jamie," I smile and throw my arms around him in a giant hug that has me lifted off the floor.

He rests me back on the black-and-white checkered tile and rests his chin on my head. "Missed you, Tink."

"I thought we were all getting together this weekend?" I ask as Maddox Beneventi, Maverick Beneventi, and the man who still haunts my dreams, Killian St. James, shuffle into my home, already talking animatedly about something with my brother.

Maverick tosses a wicked smile Jamie's way. "Yeah well, Rosie is spending the night at my parents' house this weekend. Some of us still have football games to play."

"Damn, man," Jamie growls. "Don't be a dick about it."

Jamie's team might be out of the playoffs, but Maverick plays for my Uncle Declan, and the Philadelphia Kings only have to win one more game to get to the Superbowl this year.

"Facts are facts, man. We've got a game Sunday. I can't catch up this weekend."

"How is my favorite rose?" I ask, as I kiss Mav's cheek.

His smile is huge. "She's good and she can't wait to see you, Aunt Tink."

We follow Noah into my kitchen where he tosses the guys each a bottle of beer from the freshly stocked fridge, and these giant men all spread out. "Tonight's my night off, *so . . .* what are we going to do with it?"

I drag my eyes over the enormous men. The quiet one so much bigger than the others, but then again, Killian always was. Bigger. Better looking. Wilder. He's got more ink peeking out from under his shirt than he used to, but it looks good on him. Maybe a little too good.

Asshole.

Even in high school, he towered over me, but back then, I liked it. Easily six foot five to my five foot two. Only now, his muscles stretch the fabric of his shirt, easily twice the size they used to be. His messy blond hair, a little too long, and those eyes . . . bright green, like a black cat's.

I may have written a song or two about him in high school, but that was before . . . and maybe after. He doesn't need to know that though. No one does. "You guys should go out. Have fun. You don't need me to do that." I look down at my bare legs and the white cotton boxers with red hearts that barely cover my ass, along with the bright red fuzzy socks I'm rocking, and want to die. Of course, this is how I see Killian for the first freaking time in ages. Grrr . . . I'm going to kill Noah. "I really don't feel like dealing with the paparazzi tonight."

Without any argument, Maddox drops down onto one of the kitchen chairs and pulls out his phone. "What kind of food are you in the mood for?" he asks no one in particular but smirks my way.

Jamie's arm goes back to my shoulders. "I bet you've got some hot little assistant who could get us something to eat, don't ya, Tink?"

"Guys . . . you should go out. I swear I won't be upset." *Lies.* As much as I wanted to be alone, now that they're here, I don't want them to leave. At least not all of them. "Just because I'm no fun doesn't mean you should be."

I glance at Noah, searching for what . . . I'm not sure.

Help, maybe. Backup is probably more like it.

But Noah yanks his phone from his pocket with a flourish. "Her name is Tasha, and she's smokin' hot."

"Off-limits is what he meant to say," I add, looking directly at Maddox. "She's not here for your entertainment."

The fucker laughs at me. "We'll see about that, Tink."

Noah's fingers fly across his phone as we all watch, and I cringe.

Pretty sure my quiet night just got long and loud.

Killian

Chapter 2

"*I*'m out." My cards hit the table as I throw back a shot of Don Julio and groan. "I fucking hate tequila . . ."

Lilah giggles as I push away from the table in search of water. She shakes the half-empty bottle in front of me. "Scared of a little tequila, champ?"

Her pale cheeks pink as she rolls her lips together, and *yeah* . . . my annoyance dies a little. Fuck, she's pretty. Pretty and perfect like one of those porcelain dolls my mother used to buy for my sisters. She always has been.

I guess some things never change, even if the bigger things have to.

"Listen, Tink. Some of us have to stay in shape for our jobs," Jamie teases, and Lilah's entire face blooms bright red, letting me know what's coming seconds before she smacks the back of his big head.

"Take it back," she demands and yanks his hair, forcing him to arch his head back.

"Ow. Shit." He swats her away like a fly. "Stop fucking pinching me."

Maverick pushes back from the table, getting out of the line of fire, and Lilah laughs with her beautiful smile and tugs again. "I'm not pinching you, dipshit. I'm pulling your hair." She wraps Jamie's hair around her fingers and yanks. "Now take it back."

"Dude . . ." Jamie looks at Noah, who shakes his head, then looks at me and Maddox. "Help . . ."

Maddox lifts his hands while I laugh. "Sorry, man. She's pissed at you, not me."

Lilah tugs harder. "Take it back, Jameson Murphy, or I'll tell your mother who really broke her crystal vase from the Queen of England."

"What the fuck, Tink? I was just teasing," he sputters, and I shit you not, it's the funniest thing I've seen in so damn long. Lilah Ryan is five foot nothing, and maybe all of a hundred-and-ten pounds soaking fucking wet, and in spite of her pristine image, she's vicious and curses more than most fighters I know.

Why is that hot?

She pulls again, this time forcing him to look at her. "I'll have you know I run for two hours and twenty-two minutes every single day. Every. Day. Jamie. And I sing my entire set while I'm doing it. Two hours. Do you think I could possibly pull that off if I wasn't in shape?" When he doesn't answer fast enough, she yanks again. "Don't be an asshole, Jamie."

"Sorry. *Shit*. Stop. I said sorry," he whines, and I may or may not pull my phone out to get a picture of this shit. *What can I say?* It's funny as hell, and I can think of a few people who are gonna love it.

She lets go and smacks the back of his head—*again*. "I'd like to see you sing for two hours while you're running and never lose your breath."

"Jamie doesn't run," Noah laughs.

"Or tackle," Maverick laughs, then ducks out of the way.

"Or sing," Maddox adds.

Lilah's eyes bounce between them, then look at me for what feels like the first time all night, waiting to see what I'm going to add, but it's my turn to hold my hands up in surrender. "I didn't say a word."

Her pretty blue eyes narrow.

There was a time when I knew exactly what this girl was thinking just from a single look.

But not anymore.

"Well, I may not be a professional fighter or play football like you two assholes, but I have to stay in shape for my job too, and not just because every inch of fat on my body gets scrutinized. So you can all suck it," she growls and storms into the other room, leaving the five of us in her wake.

"That was hot," I murmur, and Maddox elbows me.

Noah shakes his head and throws a bottle cap at Jamie. "Fucking moron."

"How was I supposed to know I'd hit a nerve?" Jamie asks and finishes his beer like he just saw his life pass before his eyes. "I was just kidding."

"Some asshole wrote an article about Lilah gaining weight last month, and she's been a little sensitive ever since." Noah drags his hands down his face. "We needed this break. We're fucking tired."

I'd like to get a hold of whatever dick wrote that article and use him for a practice dummy. Show him what happens when you pick on someone your own size for a change. Lilah might be tiny, but she's got curves for days. Perfect curves a man can grip.

Fuck.

"How long are you home?" Maddox asks as he tosses a few more bills to the center of the table.

Asshole always wins at poker.

"A few months, maybe. Not sure yet. We'll hammer it all out when we meet with management next week."

Jamie says something, but I tune him out and, as if tethered to her the way we were a decade ago, decide to take my life in my own hands and follow the feisty woman.

She's tucked into the corner of an L-shaped sofa with a gas fireplace crackling in front of her, the cobalt blue flames nearly the same color as her closed eyes. Huge windows dominate every wall, and her face is lifted toward the stars shining through the glass.

She's fucking stunning.

Something about her like this hits me right in the solar plexus.

We've managed to avoid each other for nearly ten years. We may have been at the same parties and functions occasionally but never in a small group. Especially not this group. In high school, it was always us. Noah, Jamie, Maverick, Lilah, and me.

She called us the four horsemen of the apocalypse. But the truth is the only war I would have rained down on anyone would have been for her.

Maybe I shouldn't have broken that streak by coming tonight. It probably wasn't my smartest move. But when Jamie called . . . *I don't know.* I just needed to see her. To make sure she was really okay after the news broke about the bomb found at the last stop on her tour. I knew what I was told. But knowing it and seeing her alive and breathing are two very different things.

None of that seems to matter as I sit down next to her. "I don't remember you being such a ballbuster in high school."

She bats her long, dark lashes up at me, and that pretty blush comes back out to play. "There're a lot of things you don't remember."

"Damn." I hold my fist over my chest. "Shots fired."

Not that she's wrong. Not completely.

She drags her eyes from the top of my head slowly down my body before her lips tilt up into the sexy smile I've seen

15

on a million different magazine covers over the years. *Practiced. Fake.* "No shots. Just the truth."

"You want the truth? Truth is I remember everything, princess." I take the bottle of tequila out of her hand, and she bristles like I knew she would.

"I hate that stupid nickname."

Knew she'd say that too.

"No, you don't." The tequila warms my throat as it goes down, and I know I'm going to regret this shit when I run tomorrow morning, but I take another shot anyway before I pass it back.

Her hair feels like silk between my fingers as I tuck a golden lock behind her ear and smile as she leans into my hand. "You never did."

For half her fucking life, I was the person she called when something went wrong or right. I was who she wanted. And fuck if I didn't love being that guy.

"Oh yeah?" she whispers. "And what makes you think that?"

"Because ballbuster or not, you're still a shit liar," I challenge.

She licks her lips and leans in a breath closer. "That's okay because it turned out you were a good enough liar for both of us."

Shit.

Guess I deserve that.

"Why are you here, Killian?"

I run my thumb along her cheek, and for a minute, it's gone. The anger. The hurt. The stupid teenage hormones. It's just Lilah and me. "Guess I wanted to see for myself that you were okay."

"I'm fine," she murmurs as she pulls back, her mask firmly in place, and I drop my hand.

Footsteps sound in the hall as Lilah stands, refusing to

16

look at me as Maddox walks in. "I'm heading back to the condo, man. You coming with?"

"Yeah. I'll be right behind you." I don't bother taking my eyes off the woman in front of me as Maddox walks back out. "One day, you're going to have to listen to me, princess."

"One day, maybe you'll say something worth listening to, champ." She turns and, unlike me, has no problem looking away as she leaves me alone.

Not the first time she's done that either.

Chapter 3

Blast the music until you can't feel a fucking thing . . .

—Lilah's Secret Thoughts

"It's my parents' house, Xander. No one is going to get to me here. Either go home or come inside and let my mother feed you." I stand outside the front door, waiting for an answer I know I'm never getting but wishing for it anyway.

Xander has been with me for two and a half years. He's a good bodyguard. Nice enough to be around and big enough that he deters most people just by looking at him. They don't know he'd rather save a fly than squish one. They also don't know he's a better shot than most secret service agents are, which is just fine with me.

He also runs a team of men who look like silent assassins.

I don't think they actually are, but they're scary enough to look like they are.

"Now, Lilah," he placates me. "You know I'm not leaving, and I already had breakfast, but thank your mom for me. I'll be right here when you're ready to leave." With his big arms crossed over his chest, he waits for me to step through the front door before he walks back to the SUV, leaving me to follow the sound of laughter.

I'm not gonna lie. I'm half surprised Mom didn't tackle me at the front door during my unsuccessful negotiation tactics.

As I stop at the edge of the kitchen and look at my family, I make a mental note to thank Noah for taking the brunt of the attention when we got here. My sister, Dillan, is sitting at the island picking at the strawberries Mom set out because she's just that good and knows they're my favorite. Asher tries to snag a berry from the bowl, and Mom smacks his hand. "Leave some for Lilah."

He looks from Dillan to Mom and back again while he groans, "What the hell?"

I take a quick minute to soak it all in. The way Dad stands with Mom tucked into his side as she shoves a plate of food Noah's way. The way Dillan looks at Noah like he hung the moon. He was always her favorite. The smell of freshly baked cinnamon raisin rolls covered in crushed walnuts from Sweet Temptations, and the way it mixes with the salty caramel coffee Mom and Dillan can't go a day without.

It smells like love and warmth and safety.

It wraps around me like the warmest, softest blanket, comforting me in the way only home can.

Home.

I couldn't wait to get out of here to go on my first tour, and after nearly a decade of what feels like non-stop touring, I'm not sure I ever want to leave again.

That simple thought has my shoulders relaxing and my ever-present anxiety taking a much-needed back seat as I make my way in and tuck myself under my father's other arm. "Hi, Daddy."

He drops a kiss on my head, and my siblings all mock me. "*Hi, Daddy.*"

Whatever. They can all suck it.

I stick my tongue out at them and giggle as Mom hugs me like an anaconda trying to strangle its prey.

"Let her breathe, Nat. You just had her home last month for Christmas." Dad's hand wraps around Mom's hip as he comes to my defense.

I swear I love my mom, but thank God for Dad or she'd smother us all.

"Fine." She takes a step back and picks up her coffee mug as she looks at me. "Honey, you look tired."

"Mom . . ." I whine. Yup. I'm home for ten minutes, and I'm already whining. So proud. "I wanted to sleep later, but you insisted on breakfast."

Dillan leans back in her stool and stares at me. "You should try eating a muffin, Tink. Your ass is looking kinda small."

"Oh my God . . . *Really?*" I smile and reach for a bottle of water. "I've added extra cardio to my workout to drop a dress size."

"Why?" Asher asks as he pushes a muffin my way. "Guys like ass, Tink."

I shake my head. "Camera adds ten pounds, Ash."

"Guys don't need to like your sister's ass," Dad scolds them both.

"You look perfect." Mom hands me a cup of hot tea. "Now tell us what's going on. Noah said you guys are meeting with the label next week to reschedule the rest of the tour. Your father and I would like to be there."

"Mom," Noah stops her before I have the chance. "We've got this."

But we both know there's no stopping Natalie Ryan. "You both need extra security. I don't care if your label provides it or if we have to. But you need it before you agree to go back out."

"Mom . . ." he tries again, but this time the look she gives him stops him before he can say anything else. "They don't give a shit about me. Lilah needs it more than I do."

"Fucking traitor," I croak, and he has the decency to cringe.

"It's true." Dillan holds her phone up and scrolls through multiple articles. "For every article I've seen that includes Noah since the tour was canceled, I've seen ten more that only mention you. It was *your* dressing room, Lilah."

Dad wraps his big arm around my shoulders and squeezes, relaxing me in a way only he can. Brady Ryan may have retired from football nearly fifteen years ago, but he's as strong as he's ever been. When he started coaching the football team at our old high school, he used to do half the workouts with the guys. They still bust his balls about all the up-downs he made them do.

"Is that why we're here? Is this some kind of security intervention?" I can't help my defensive tone. "I'm sorry. I know you're coming at this from a good place, but this week has been hell, and I just don't think I have it in me to talk about all of it yet."

The tears I refuse to cry burn the backs of my lids.

Three days ago, we walked into our biggest stop of the *Captivating* tour and were five feet from my dressing room when security rushed me out, only to find out fifteen minutes later that a bomb disguised as a gift had been delivered earlier that afternoon. Security found it during their sweep.

No one knows who the package came from or when.

They have no idea who sent it or why.

Just that if it had gone off, it could have killed hundreds or maybe thousands of people.

Thinking about it sends a chill down my spine and makes my stomach churn.

How many innocent people could have been hurt because someone was trying to get to me? I lift my tea with a shaking hand. "I know you mean well—"

"Lilah, we don't mean well," Mom interrupts. "We're terrified."

"That call . . ." Dad starts with a gravelly voice, then clears his throat. "I hope to God you never have to get that kind of a call from your children. Nothing, and I mean nothing, has ever shaken me to my core the way that call did. Tink, you've got to understand, your mom and I *get* high-profile. We understand it in a way most people can't. We've both been there. This entire family has lived it. But you've taken that to new heights we've never had to deal with, and we're learning as we go here. These last few years have taken you away from us and given you to the world, and we don't know how to protect you in this new rarefied air. But I'll be damned if we don't figure it out. For both of you."

I look across the island to Noah. His head is tilted to the side like he's trying to figure out a chord that just doesn't sound right, and I know a split-second before he opens his mouth that he's about to give in. "You're right." His dark blue eyes beg me to understand. "What do you think we need to do?"

I open my mouth to argue, but the pleading look on Dad's face is enough to break me. He's never scared. Never. He never loses his cool. He's the calmest person I've ever seen under pressure. But this scared him. I lean further into his side and look around the room. "I'm sorry. I wasn't trying to be selfish. I just hate having security around twenty-four seven. I love my life, but I miss my freedom. You're right. I'm not sure what's going to happen next, but until this all dies down, we need to be better prepared."

"We'll figure it out together," Mom offers softly. "But so help me, if your label can't guarantee your safety, you are not going back out on tour, even if it means I have to lock you both in your old bedrooms."

"They can just shimmy out of the window like Asher's girlfriend does." Dillan pops a berry in her mouth and purses her lips toward Asher, challenging him to say she's wrong.

"Again, it's not like I'm the twenty-two-year-old still living at home with Mommy and Daddy."

"Whatever." She flips him off and slides her phone across the counter. "How about starting with self-defense classes? Uncle Coop is teaching a class at Crucible. He's been bugging me to come."

"That's a great idea," Mom chimes in, and I fight my knee-jerk reaction that I'd rather it be anywhere else but there. Especially after last night.

"He's got one later today," Dillan adds, and I bite down on my lower lip so hard, I'm surprised blood doesn't trickle down my chin.

Crucible.

Killian St. James's gym.

The one his father owns, where I have no doubt Killian trains. Daily.

Shit.

"Damn it. I'm meeting with my editor this afternoon. But you two should go," Mom pushes. "I've already talked to Cooper about the security system at your new house."

"We don't have to," I tell her, dying for an excuse to delay the inevitable. "I mean, we could wait for you."

"Please . . ." Dillan mocks. "It will be way easier to check out the hot fighters training if you're not there, Mom."

Dad lifts a brow, and Noah smothers a laugh. "You going to learn how to keep attackers away or how to pick up a man, Dillan?"

She smiles my way. "Both."

"Take Xander with you," Dad warns, and my heart sinks. They didn't push Xander on me like this last month when I was home, and I'm not sure how I'm going to deal with it now.

There's safety, then there's suffocating.

"Thanks for coming with me, Tink. I really wanted to do this, but I didn't want to do it alone," Dillan muses as Xander turns off Main Street, and a pang of guilt hits me hard. I'm a shitty sister. Noah and I have always been thick as thieves. It's what happens when you spend nine months in a womb with someone. We've been inseparable our whole lives. We're also a few years older than Dillan, so she's always been just a little left behind. Even before we left for our first tour.

I think I need to take whatever time off I'm about to be handed and maybe fix the distance the past few years have cemented between us. "Why would you have to do it alone? None of your friends would have come with you?"

She shrugs and looks out the window as we pull into Crucible's parking lot. "They're working."

Shit. The all too familiar gesture makes me think I've just hit a nerve.

"I should be thanking you. I think agreeing to do this got Mom off my back for now," I admit and look at the familiar building in front of us.

Crucible.

This gym holds a ton of memories. The boys spent so much time here in high school, which meant I did too . . .

Good memories. Memories of them sparring on the mats while I sat against the wall writing songs—and maybe trying to hide the fact that it was harder to write every single time Killian took his shirt off.

No sixteen-year-old boy was supposed to be that defined, and I wasn't the only one who noticed. Every girl in school did. Even a few who had already graduated noticed because when you're Killian St. James, of course the college girls are interested, even though you're a lowly high schooler.

Fucker.

"Don't kid yourself. Mom isn't going to back off until she knows you and Noah are safe." Dillan hops out of the SUV, and I try to ignore the butterflies taking flight in my stomach the closer I get to the gym doors.

When Xander's door slams shut behind me, I nail him with a glare. "My uncle is teaching the class, and he's a former Navy SEAL, Xander. I guarantee I'm safe in there."

"Lilah—"

"Xander . . . Please. Just give me some room to breathe." I drop my voice, so Dillan can't hear me. "I'm literally begging you. I need some space, or I'm going to suffocate."

He stares at me, unflinching, and I cringe.

"You really going to come inside?" I ask, pissed. This is ridiculous.

One eyebrow shoots up in answer, and I turn away and hurry to catch up with Dillan.

"Lurch coming in with us?" Dillan looks less than thrilled.

"Lurch? Who the hell is Lurch?"

"You know . . ." She yanks on the front door of Crucible and looks at me. "The big dude from *The Addams Family*. Lurch."

When I don't respond, she shakes her head in frustration. "Is he at least going to stay quiet and far away?"

I hear the question, but any answer I have gets stuck in

my throat as I'm assaulted by memories of the last time I was here.

Hands on my face and fury in his eyes.

Like he had any right to be furious.

"Hey, girls." Uncle Cooper interrupts my trip down memory lane before the wreckage can break me. "Your mom told me you were coming today." He drops a kiss on the top of my head, then Dillan's. "How long are you home, Lilah?"

"I'm not sure yet. I'll find out next week." I scan the giant room, completely blindsided by how much this place looks exactly the same, before my eyes stop on the cage. "Oh . . ."

Killian stands outside the cage like a gorgeous warrior god in his gym shorts and his hands wrapped. Sweat glistens on his enormously muscled bare chest, and my mouth waters.

Cooper looks behind him with a knowing smirk as Killian slips a white t-shirt on.

Shame . . .

"Don't be intimidated by Killer, girls. He's going to be helping us with class today."

"What?" I snap, and Dillan giggles.

"I volunteer as tribute," she murmurs, and Uncle Cooper ignores her.

"Is that your bodyguard, Lilah?" He looks less than impressed when I nod. "Is he any good?"

"Well, he wouldn't stay outside," Dillan answers for me.

"Good. He shouldn't. You need someone good, Tink. I'll check him out and let you know if he's it." Uncle Cooper left the SEALs forever ago and mainly manages money now. But we all know he does more than that. Elite stuff he'll never admit. I'd sure hate to be the person who pisses him off.

I feel eyes on me. Bright green eyes that sear my skin and hurt my heart.

Damn him.

Refusing to acknowledge those eyes or the way I know they're moving closer, I smile at Uncle Coop. "So, am I going to be able to kick someone's ass after this class?"

"It's self-defense, princess. You're not learning to fight. You're learning to defend yourself." That voice. Grr . . .

I throw an elbow back into Killian's stomach the way he taught me when we were ten, and I think my elbow may have just hit a brick wall. One that humors me with an *oof*, even though there's no way I did any damage.

"Not bad, Lilah. Now go warm up while I have a quick chat with your bodyguard." Uncle Coop points us to the thick black mats in the corner of the room.

Uncle Coop crosses the room, and Killian grunts, "Your bodyguard looks like he'd be quicker to chase a donut than stop a threat, princess."

"Princess," Dillan gasps. "Interesting."

"Not interesting," I correct her and level him with a glare. I seem to be handing them out left and right today. "Annoying is more like it."

Killian's lips curve into a wicked grin. "Just saying, Lilah . . ." He overly annunciates my name just to prove a big, fat, stupid point. "But that dude doesn't look like he'd be any good at guarding your body."

His smile is replaced by anger, and I want to throw my hands up in the air in defeat or frustration.

There was a time I wanted nothing more than for this man in front of me to be the man *guarding my body*. Now the thought pisses me off. "Guess it's a good thing you don't have to be concerned with who's guarding my body then."

Dillan whistles, and I take that as my cue to walk away.

The Philly Press

IN IT TO WIN IT

What do you get when you take one team on fire and send them the biggest game of the year? You get a celebration, and with a celebration comes hot athletes taking to our city streets and bars in droves. And this reporter is here for it. Check back soon to see the who's who and where's where of our favorite Philly Kings players this week.

#KroydonKronicles #SuperBowlBound #InItToWinIt

Killian

Chapter 4

NOAH

Who wants to grab a beer?

JAMIE

I'm in. Where to?

MADDOX

I'm working tonight.

MAVERICK

West End it is.

JAMIE

Good. Drinks are on Maverick.

MAVERICK

WTF?

JAMIE

Come on . . . We've got to celebrate you going to the Superbowl.

MAVERICK

Shouldn't drinks be on you then, asswipe?

JAMIE

Fuck no. You're getting a Superbowl bonus. My season's over.

KILLIAN

I'm in, but I can't drink.

NOAH

Looks like Killer's driving.

JAMIE

Is Lilah coming?

NOAH

Doubt it. The only time she's left the house is to go to the gym or my parents' house.

MAVERICK

Should we force her out?

NOAH

Nah. She'd be pissed.

MADDOX

Lilah's even hotter when she's pissed.

NOAH

Gross, dude.

MADDOX

She's not my sister.

I ignore whatever else the guys say and shove my phone back in my pocket.

Pretty sure I've never wanted to punch Maddox as much as I do right at this moment.

Lilah *is* hot when she's pissed, and it's so much fun to piss her off. It's easy too.

She's been at Crucible every day since the self-defense class . . . showing up in skintight leggings and a crop top. Or worse, skintight booty shorts and a sports bra. Smiling at everyone inside. Everyone but me. Me, she glares at. Full-on fucking glares.

Her curves are softer than most of the female fighters we have training. Her muscles not quite as defined but still there. A hidden strength.

She won't come near me. Just runs on the treadmill or attacks the StairMaster with her headphones on, humming or singing while she's at it.

And the girl barely breaks a sweat.

It's more like a glow.

A fucking glow.

"You talking to yourself, baby brother?" My older sister, Brynlee, walks into her office and kicks the door shut behind her. She's been the physical therapist at Crucible for a few years now, and honestly, I love having her here . . . *usually*. "Up on the table, Killian. Let me see that shoulder."

I hop up on the table and shrug out of my shirt so she can manipulate my muscles. My shoulder has been giving me a hard time for a few days, and with the fight two months away, that's a problem.

"So . . . why were you talking to yourself?" Her thumb digs in, pressing on a pressure point near the joint, and I wince.

"I wasn't—ow! Shit, Brynn . . ."

"Don't be a baby." Her eyes narrow as she moves her thumbs and positions her baby bump away from the table. "And I call bullshit. You've got a look, and you were mumbling . . ." She slides her fingers over the ball of my shoulder. "What's going on?"

"Nothing." She pushes harder, and I wince again. "Christ, Brynnie. If I wanted you to know, I'd have been talking to you instead of myself."

"No, you wouldn't." She pushes me until my back hits the table, then works her way down my arm. "Fine. Keep it to yourself. But don't think we haven't all noticed you've been distracted lately."

"Have not."

"Now you sound like my kids, Killer." She hooks me up to the stim machine and takes a step back. " Any chance it has something to do with a certain Ryan girl?"

I ignore her.

Wrong move.

"I knew it. You've got a thing for Dillan Ryan."

My head whips her way. "I don't. But nice try."

"Lilah?" This time she sounds more shocked and less excited. "Damn, little brother."

"I don't have a thing for Lilah Ryan. We're friends."

There's no way she believes that line of bullshit. We haven't been friends in years, and she knows it, but she doesn't call me out on it either. "Whatever you say. But keep your head in the game. Dad will have your ass if you get distracted now."

"Yeah . . . I know." But even as I agree, my mind drifts to Lilah and those leggings.

I'm so fucking screwed.

"$\mathcal{H}$ ow's training going, man?" Noah taps his beer to my water and pulls his hat down lower over his eyes as the two of us sit, nearly hidden, in the back corner of Maddox's bar while Jamie dances with a few of the Kings cheerleaders.

I hold my water up again. "It's going. Living like a monk. So, you know . . ."

"Nah, man. Not really sure I know how that one goes," he laughs. Noah may have been quieter about it than the rest of us, but he's been just as big a partier as all of us have. "But it sounds pretty shitty."

"When I defend my title next month and win, it'll be worth it." I tell myself the same damn thing every day . . . when Dad and Hudson are giving me shit. When I'm shoveling down chicken and rice for the fifteenth day in a row. When everyone else is enjoying a beer and I'm sucking down water. "What the hell is going on with your living arrangements? Did you get moved back into your place? Or are you subletting it to Jamie?"

He takes a pull from his beer as the entire dance floor erupts when the song changes and Lilah's beautiful voice sings "You Never Knew Me At All." He cringes and moves further into the shadows. "That's not what you want to ask me, Killer."

It's not.

Noah's asked me what happened between Lilah and me more than once, but he never pushes it when I don't answer him. He's a good friend, but he's her twin brother. That trumps good friend. He knew how close we were before they left for their first tour. And he knows we're not now. And he's never assumed I was some asshole who hurt her. I respect the hell out of that. So I ask him the same thing I always do. "How is she?"

"She's stressed and tired and burned the hell out. We told the label we weren't ready to go on tour last summer, but they own us for now, so we didn't have a whole lot of say in it."

"That it?" I push, not sure if I'm ready to hear the answer.

"She's scared, man. Whether she'll admit it to herself or not, she's freaking out, and I'm worried. What happened . . . it was just . . . Fuck. It was too close." He drags his hand down his face and looks away. "I'm worried about her."

Lilah is the most fearless girl I've ever known. I hate to think of her being scared because she'll never admit it. It's not in her DNA.

"That why you've been staying there instead of at your place?"

"Yeah. But I'm going back to my place tomorrow." He finishes his beer and pushes the empty toward Maddox, who's stopped on the other side of the bar. "She figured out what I was doing and was pissed."

Maddox drops three shot glasses in front of us, then takes a two-thousand-dollar bottle of bourbon off his shelf and holds it up.

"Fuck, Madman . . ." I nod because there's no way I'm saying no to that bourbon, but I'm gonna be sweating this shit out tomorrow.

My friends are bad influences.

Does that work once you're past twelve years old?

Sorry I sucked wind on the mats today. My friends pressured me.

Dad would laugh my ass out of Crucible after he kicked it across his cage.

"Why are you two assholes hiding in the corner?" He pours three shots but keeps them in front of himself while he waits for an answer.

"Just not in the mood to deal with everyone. Lilah and I are meeting with the label tomorrow, and I wanted to get the hell out of the house tonight." He takes one of the shots from Maddox. "Not really looking for more than a good drink with old friends."

"You remember when we drank your dad's bourbon and filled it back up with water?" I snag another one of the glasses and laugh. "Dude, I thought your dad was going to kick our asses."

35

"I was grounded for a month," Noah groans, and I can't stop picturing Lilah sitting on their couch in my Kroydon Hills wrestling hoodie while she laughed and warned us we were going to get caught.

She was right. She was always right.

Maddox looks at the two of us like we're fucking crazy and picks up the remaining shot. "Told you it was a dumb move, and you idiots were going to get caught."

"To being young and dumb," I toast, and we all tap glasses and throw back the bourbon.

It goes down smooth like honey.

Madman pours another round and grins. "Don't pussy out on me, Killer."

"Fuck, man . . ." I pick up the glass and know I'm screwed.

We shoot another round, and if it's possible, it goes down easier than the last.

I slam my empty glass on the counter and wait for Noah to look at me. "So what are you gonna do?"

"About what?" Maddox asks.

"Lilah," I fill in.

"You worried about her security? I saw that fat-ass bodyguard at the gym the other day. Seriously. Where'd you find him, and why aren't you using one of my dad's guys?" Madman wipes the bar in front of him and blows off the hot redhead trying to get his attention. "Her dude doesn't look like he's going to keep her safe."

"The label hired him," is all Noah says.

"Fire him and hire someone good," Maddox argues. "Fuck. From what I hear, she needs someone closer than she's letting him get anyway."

Noah's head snaps up. "Who are you hearing that from?"

"I have my ways," Maddox reassures him without answering the question and moves down the bar to help a group of college girls.

Typical Madman.

"We'll see what the label says tomorrow. Lilah doesn't even want one while she's in town." Noah's voice is defeated. He sounds as tired as he says his sister is. "She's pushing back every chance she can get. Won't even let him in the house."

"Fuck the label," I bark. "You guys should be the ones to decide the best way to keep her safe."

"I'm telling you, Killer. She doesn't want any of it. She thinks she can still walk down Main Street by herself and be safe."

"Goddamn. She's always been so stubborn," I growl and ignore the way he looks at me.

"You're the only one she used to listen to. Maybe you should take a stab at it."

"Ha . . . That's funny. Lilah would rather *stab me* than listen to anything I say now." Fuck if it isn't true and if that doesn't suck.

"Yeah . . . but you'd keep her safe." It's like a lightbulb just went off behind his eyes. "You could be there when I'm not. And . . . you could be inside the house. She won't let Xander in."

"What are you talking about? What's a Xander?" I swear to God, he's only had two beers and two shots, but he's already losing me as his train of thought zigzags along.

"Xander is her bodyguard. He may not look like much, but he's a perfect shot."

Maddox hears the word *shot* a few steps down the bar and pops his head back in front of us. "Like with a gun?"

Guess now he's intrigued.

Noah nods. "Ten out of ten."

"Doubtful," Madman muses. "Bet I could take him."

"Lilah doesn't want some guy whipping out a gun to protect her. That should be the last option." My voice thunders a little more than it should, but she hates guns. Hates them. "There's about ten million ways to protect someone before you have to reach for a weapon."

Noah and Maddox seem to have a whole conversation without saying a word before they look at me with eerie fucking smiles that creep me the hell out. "Whatever you're thinking, stop."

"Dude." Noah points at me with his bottle of beer. "You're the answer."

"The answer to what?" I think I know what he's about to say, but it's like I can't steer away from the impending disaster.

"You . . . You can keep her safe. You can stay in the house. She can go to the gym with you during the day—" Noah seems thrilled with this idea as Maddox cuts him off.

"Yeah, and nobody would think anything of it if you were out with her. This guy everyone is so worried about thinks he's in love with her. Show him he can't have her. You could be her boyfriend. You know . . . friends to lovers. High-school sweethearts. All that shit," Maddox adds, and I stare in shock.

"What?" I ask, and neither guy answers. Fuck. They don't even look at me until I slam my palm against the bar. "What the fuck are you talking about? Who loves her? What guy?"

"How'd you know?" Noah asks Maddox grimly.

Madman lifts his chin, but his knuckles grow white against his grip on the bar. "I make it my business to know when my friends are threatened. I'm a goddamn Beneventi. You really surprised?"

Fuck. He's pissed. And I'm not following.

"Someone want to clue me the hell in?" It's a demand as much as a question.

"The bomb." Noah's elbows hit the bar, and he buries his head in his hands. "She had a stalker for about two months before that. One who likes to send her *things*. He thinks he loves her. He thinks she loves him. The note said everyone was keeping her away from him, and he didn't want anyone in the way."

My lungs forget how to pump air, and I choke on the weight of what he just said.

A stalker.

The last time someone I knew had a stalker, someone died.

Suddenly, I stop worrying about breathing and concentrate on not puking up my shots.

"That doesn't make sense. If Lilah knows about this freak, why is she fighting so hard against having security?" But even as I say the words, the answer smacks me in the face as hard as Maddox's fist when we're sparring. "Shit." I stare between Noah and Maddox. "She doesn't know."

It's not a question.

I know I'm right before I look at Noah's guilty-as-fuck face.

"How the hell could she not know?" I demand.

Noah blows out a long breath. "I'm not even sure how *he* knows. But I just figure I'm better off not asking."

Yeah. I get that. We all just let Maddox do his thing and accept it with few questions.

"But Lilah. How could she not know?" My head throbs at the idea of them hiding this from her.

"The label kept it quiet. No one knows. I only know because I may have had a thing going with our tour manager. Seriously, man. I just found out when it all happened. I haven't even told our parents yet." Noah looks torn. "I don't know what the hell I'm doing. But having someone there who could protect her . . ."

"She fucking hates me," I groan and crack my neck. "What the hell am I supposed to do? Force my way into her home?"

I mean, I could. It could work.

Who's gonna fuck with her with a world heavyweight champion fighter at her side?

What's the alternative?

"She didn't always hate you . . ." Noah reminds me, and Maddox laughs.

The asshole pushes another beer across the counter, and I shake my head, refusing it. This whole thing . . . whole night is a bad idea. "She sure hates you now though."

I glare at Madman.

Yeah, she does.

He slams the lid of the beer against the bar and drinks it himself. "You know what they say about love and hate?"

"There's a thin line," I grumble.

"I was gonna say the sex is better with hate," Madman grins, and Noah gags.

"No sex. I wasn't whoring her out," Noah blows out, and I shove him away.

"Don't talk about whores and Lilah in the same fucking sentence, asshole," I warn him, and his smug smile makes me wish I'd hit him harder.

Noah smacks my shoulder and throws a hundred down on the bar. "Sounds like we better get you home, Killer. You've got some convincing to do."

"What?" Goddammit, this is a bad idea.

He adjusts his hat lower on his head and looks around. "You got a back door we can leave through, Madman?"

Maddox tips his head past the bar, and I stand, wondering if I actually just agreed to this crazy idea. I grab Noah's shoulder and shove him toward the back hall and Maddox's office. "You sure this is a good idea?"

I'm not sure what I want to hear more . . . yes or no.

One forces Lilah and me together again after years of distance, and the other one doesn't.

Is it better to let what we were die in the past?

Then I think about everything Noah just laid out and realize it never did die. She might drive me batshit fucking crazy, but Lilah Ryan will always matter to me. Her safety. Her happiness. Her smile.

I'd still rain down war for her.

Lilah

I once heard female dragonflies will fake their own deaths instead of mating with unwanted males, and now I can't help but imagine them looking at their friends, laughing. Like, here comes Joey. Quick, girl, play dead.

—Lilah's Secret Thoughts

I run my fingers over the keys of my baby-grand piano, humming my favorite song. It was always one of Mom's most loved, and as I sing the first lines, I can picture her dancing in the studio in our basement. Her eyes closed, just feeling the music.

Music can transform you.

It can calm you and excite you and heal you and break you all in one really good song.

The rhythm, the beat, the heart.

If you're lucky, it's always with you. In your head and your soul.

Keeping you safe and sound and sane.

Not that I feel sane or sound or safe.

Nope. I've been robbed. Metaphorically speaking.

I've spent the better part of the past twelve months having this house built. Painstakingly picking out every last detail. From the beautiful black-and-white checkered tile floor in my music room, to the trim work on the walls, and every single oversized window that looks out onto the ten acres surrounding my house. Acres and acres of Christmas trees because I wanted open windows and open porches and open balconies with beautiful French doors. But I also wanted privacy. I wanted escapism, and this house, to me, is escapism at its finest. I get to be free and private and not feel like I'm constantly being watched and judged while also feeling like I'm not being boxed in.

What a joke. I've been put in a box my whole life.

I know. Poor little rich girl. The oldest daughter of one of the best quarterbacks the NFL has ever seen and one of the most successful romance authors to ever put her fingers against a keyboard. Must have been a really hard life.

Truth be told, it wasn't.

It was idyllic.

How many people can say they grew up in a happy, loving, well-adjusted family, with two parents who loved them and each other? We like to tease Mom and Dad that maybe they love each other a little too much. But really, seeing the way Dad still likes to squeeze Mom's ass when he thinks we're not watching gives me hope that I'll have that one day. Though, I could go the rest of my life without over-hearing them doing whatever they like to do when they sneak away, which is whenever they think they can get away with it. Good lord, who knew you could be that hot for each other after almost thirty years? Yup. Thirty. They were high-school sweethearts too.

I used to think that would be me.

The high-school sweethearts who grew old together.

I mean . . . that's what I thought when I was fifteen. It

took me a year to put it out there to see if the sweetheart I loved felt the same. I thought he did. I still think the fucker did. But for such a badass, scary guy, apparently love and commitment are the two things that scared him. That would explain all the other girls he *noticed* in school. I was his best friend. I was who he hung out with. I was the one cheering him on at his wrestling meets and MMA tournaments. We were study buddies. We were confidants. We were everything. But it turns out, we were actually nothing at all.

We were everything until we were nothing at all.

That's not too bad.

I grab my phone and sing the lyric into my app before jotting it down into my notes. My fingers sliding over the keys again, this time to the melody playing in my head. The one rudely interrupted when the front door opens, jolting me momentarily until I hear my brother's laughter.

I grab my hoodie and toss it on over my tank, padding my way down the hall to the front door, then stop short, expecting to see Noah walking in. Not prepared for Killian to be next to him.

"Don't you have a house?" I ask before I hear how nasty it sounds. Nasty, even for me.

Killian stands tall, his broad shoulders taking up the entire doorframe as Noah pushes past him. "I have a penthouse. Thanks. Would you rather I let Noah drive home after a few too many drinks, princess?"

Noah coughs the fakest cough ever and walks toward me. "Just hear him out, Tink. I'm going to bed."

"What?" Killian and I both ask as my brother slaps us both on the back.

"You,"—he points at Killian—"work it out." Then he turns my way, his blue eyes softening. "And you . . ." Noah runs his hands up my arms. "Try listening to him for a change. Really listen, Tink. Because it's your life, and we're running out of options." He drops a kiss on the top of my head and walks up the winding staircase, gripping the wrought-iron banister like he's afraid he'll fall to his death without it.

I shift on my feet and watch Noah until he's out of sight. Because I don't know what else to do or say, I stay silent until the quiet snick of my front door locking behind Killian before he turns my way knocks me from my frozen trance. "What in the world is he talking about?"

I nearly get lost watching Killian's Adam's apple working as he swallows, then licks his lips. I don't even think he realizes what he's doing. His eyes take in every inch of my bare legs but stop on my . . . chest. What the hell?

I snap my fingers in front of his face. "My eyes are up here, champ."

"Nice hoodie." His voice is thick and delicious. Raspy.

This is why I avoid him.

These kinds of thoughts are not an option.

"It's a million years old. Why are you still here?" I fold my arms over my chest, which if I'm honest, does little to take his eyes off my boobs because I've just pushed them up. Dillan might have gotten Mom's ass, but I got her boobs.

"I know exactly how old it is, Tink. It's mine," he growls.

I roll my eyes and hold my ground. "Possession is nine-tenths of the law, and I stole this from you in ninth grade. I've had it longer than you ever did. It's mine."

"Possession, huh?" Damn that voice. Why does he sound turned-on, and why in the world does that thought do things to me? Killian walks by me like this is his house, not mine, and heads back to the kitchen.

I stand here, dumbfounded for a hot second, then yes, I

stomp my foot like a pissed-off toddler. I probably look a whole lot like my best friend's daughter right now, but I push that thought aside and follow the big oaf. "Where do you think you're going?"

Damn him and his long legs.

He's already in the kitchen with the fridge open by the time I get there. "Killian, stop."

His stupid dirty-blond head pops up above my giant subzero refrigerator door. "What. Are. You. Doing. Here?"

He holds up a bottle of water and shuts the door. "Getting water. I've got to run in the morning, and I had a shot tonight . . . Actually, two. I need to flush it from my system before I run."

"It's snowing out. You're going to run in the snow?" I can't decide if that sounds fun or stupid. Knowing me, I'd fall and bust my ass. Knowing him, he'd be fine.

Douchebag.

"You know those things at the gym that you run on . . . they're called treadmills, and I run on them too. If it weren't already snowing tonight, I'd still run outside tomorrow. But I don't want to bite it on black ice. So the gym it is. Tomorrow is a ten-mile day."

"Damn . . . ten miles, huh?" Easy peasy. But I don't tell him that.

I don't tell him anything.

"Okay. I meant what are you doing in my kitchen? Don't you have a perfectly good one at home? Your home?"

Killian cracks the lid open on the water, and here I go watching that stupid Adam's apple working again. When did this turn into my kink?

Oh yeah. When it's him.

He's always been my kink, and fucking hell, that frustrates me.

Once he finishes the bottle, he looks around for the trash,

then opens cabinets until he finds it and tosses the bottle into the recycling bin. In two big steps, he's in front of me, and in a move that has me gasping, the giant, brooding bastard puts both hands on my hips and sits me on the marble counter. His hands stay planted on either side of me. We're still not eye to eye, because when I say giant, I mean well over a foot taller than me.

"We've got to talk, princess." His words and voice hold no room for argument. He's serious, not playing, and I'm not ready for this. Not even a decade later.

"No, we don't." I slap my hand against his chest, but he doesn't budge.

This close, everything about this man is overwhelming.

The way he still smells like the ocean, even though we live an hour away from the nearest one. The catlike green eyes with the gorgeous golden flecks that only ever come out to play when he's super serious or super scared . . . rare as the second option is. His dirty-blond hair, that's always been just a little too long, that I used to run my fingers through when he'd lay his head in my lap. Ugh.

"Yeah, we do. Why are you fighting your security?"

"What?" Of all the things he could say, that wasn't what I was expecting.

"Noah told me you won't let your security do its job. He's scared to death for you. He thinks you need someone closer than you're letting them get."

When I refuse to look into his eyes, one hand slips under my chin, forcing my face up. "Lilah . . ."

"You don't get to ask me this. You don't get a say in how I live my life, Killian. You lost that privilege when you chose wrong." Emotions long ago shoved far away crawl up my throat until I push them right back down.

I will not cry over this man.

Not again. Not ever again.

"Wrong answer, Lilah."

I slide my leg up and press my bare foot to the center of his chest. "Back the fuck off before I make you, St. James. You lost privileges ten years ago. You don't get to be concerned. You don't get to have a say. And you certainly don't get to lecture me."

He wraps his rough, calloused hand around my ankle, and instead of me pushing him away, he drags me closer.

Damn it.

"Your brother is worried. Your family. Your friends. Your label. Everyone is worried about you. Everyone but you. Do you hear how selfish that sounds, Lilah? Do you?"

I yank my foot away, and anger and humiliation skitter over my skin. "Fuck you, Killian. You didn't care then, and you don't get to care now."

"I never stopped caring, princess. Believe it or not." His stupid lips tug up on one side, and he drops his hold. "Noah and Maddox both think you need a new level of security, and according to them, so do your parents."

"Oh my God," I yell. "Why the hell do you care? Jesus, I hate you."

When I shove him away this time, he lets me, and I hop down from the counter, desperate for space. But of course, that's not Killian's way. He immediately crowds me against the counter, refusing to let me escape. "Yeah well, you used to love me. I hope your acting is still top-notch. Because we have a plan, and it's going to require you to fake it till you make it, princess."

"I swear to God, if someone in the house doesn't start making sense tonight, I'm going to kick everyone's asses," I yell and smack his chest, his big, broad, solid chest that just absorbs my hit without a single move. I used to love falling asleep on that chest.

Stupid fucking muscles.

Stupid fucking man.

"I'd like to see you try." He brings his face down to my level, and his breath smells like a mix of mint and bourbon. He smells delicious. That's it. God hates me. I must have tortured kittens in a past life or something. Because there is no other reason this man should look this good this close.

"Just spit it out so you can go the hell home, St. James. I'm tired." Not a lie.

Killian wraps two strong arms around me, and for a second, I drop my forehead to his chest. This was us. The old us. The comfortable us.

I think I must be losing my ever-loving mind. Because I swear this man—the one I'm still considering kneeing in the balls—sniffs me. He inhales, and his whole body loosens. Relaxes. And mine wants to do the same. But there's no way I'm missing my chance.

I slide under his arm and dart across the kitchen, then spin on my heels, because there's no way in hell I'm giving this man my back. "You done yet?"

His responding smile is slow and wicked and so damn sexy, I'm pretty sure my panties get damp and my knees get week.

Fuck my life.

"You need a bodyguard, princess. One you'll let inside your home. One who can stick close. One who can make the whole world think you're taken." Then the bastard lifts a brow, and a dimple pops deep in his stupid cheek. Just one dimple. Because when God gave this man anything, he gave with both freaking hands. "One who doesn't have to rely on a gun to do it. And who can make a man shit his pants just by his reputation alone."

"Are you fucking kidding me?" I'm not even yelling now. Nope. I'm screaming. Like a banshee, my mother would say. A crazy, wild, fucking banshee. "Get out."

49

I march back to the front door and thank the stars above that his big black boots make even bigger, louder noises as he follows me. "You do not get to tell me what I need. And you certainly don't get to be the answer to anything I may want or not want. I'm the only one who makes decisions about my life. I'm not that sixteen-year-old girl begging you for anything, Killian, and I haven't been for a long time. Now. Get. Out."

He shoves his hands in the pockets of a hunter-green wool coat that looks unfortunately good on him, and damn, if his ridiculously cocky smile doesn't double in size. "We'll see about that, princess."

I watch in shock as he finally walks through my door and of course manages to get a foot in the way when I attempt to slam it in his ugly—how I wish it was ugly—face.

"I'll see you tomorrow, Lilah."

"In your dreams, Killian." He moves his foot and pulls the door closed behind me, robbing me of the chance to slam it. And as my blood absolutely boils, his voice echoes through the door.

"Lock up, Lilah."

Ahhhh . . .

I throw the deadbolt and set the alarm, then throw my head back against the wall and close my eyes.

"Good girl," comes through the damn door, and I want to curse him out all over again, but that would mean admitting I was still here and heard him in the first place. "'Night, princess."

I slide down the wall to my ass and almost silently whisper back, "'Night, champ."

I don't fear being alone. I fear being in a room surrounded by people I don't trust.

—Lilah's Secret Thoughts

I made sure I was out of the house this morning before Noah woke up, not wanting to test my loyalty and love for my brother. Because I swear to everything I love, I may have killed him if I had to see him before I had caffeine, and then I'd have had to deal with my mother. Instead, I snuck out like a child. Not gonna lie either, it made me happier than I've been since I got home. And when my best friend opens her front door, her baby girl, Lennox, on her hip and a look of exhaustion on her face, I know it was worth it.

"Lilah— What are you doing here? Oh my goodness, did we have plans?" Addie pushes the door open and steps aside for me to walk in, and as I do, she tracks the goodies I picked up from Sweet Temptations on my way over here. "If that's coffee, I may just leave your cousin for you."

"You are pretty hot," I giggle and triumphantly hold up

the cup carrier. "Coffee for you, tea for me, and chocolate chip muffins for both of us because I may need to eat my feelings this morning."

"That's it. Screw Leo. I'm yours."

I scoop Lennox out of her arms and inhale her sweet baby scent as she smacks my cheeks and opens her mouth for a sloppy, wet kiss. "Hey, baby girl. Did you miss me?"

"Not as much as her momma did." Addie lifts the first lid, sees that it's tea and frowns as she hands it to me before she happily picks up her own cup. "How are you holding up?"

I bounce back and forth until I've got Lennox giggling, then look over at her momma. "Ask me again in a few hours after we meet with the label."

"That's today?" She sits down at the kitchen table, sets out two napkins, and places a muffin on each one. "Is that in town or in New York?"

"In town. They have studio space in New York, but their main offices are still on the outskirts of Kroydon Hills. It's why they noticed me in the first place. Local girl making way too much noise to ignore." They had no chance. I was determined to make them notice. Refused to accept anything less. And once they did, I had them. I was the fifth act that signed to their label, and now it's one of the biggest labels in the world.

They helped me, and I helped them.

We've grown together.

But if we can't come to an agreement, there's no way I'll be signing a new contract when mine runs out.

I break off a piece of muffin, and Lennox opens her mouth. "Umm . . . can baby girl have muffin?"

"She shouldn't have sugar yet, but Leo doesn't listen, so you might as well give up the goods. He spoils her." She talks about my cousin with such adoration in her voice that my heart feels full. They haven't had the easiest road, but after the hell they went through last month, everything seems to have calmed down, and even exhausted, she looks genuinely happy.

"Where is my cousin?" I ask as I place the tiniest piece of muffin in Lennox's mouth, laughing as she gums it with a toothless grin.

"Away game," is all the answer she needs to give. Leo and his brothers, Hendrix and Nixon, are all professional hockey players. My family is full of athletes. Football players, hockey players, dancers . . . and then there's me. The dreamer. That's what they always called me. Everyone else in the family played some kind of sport at some point in their lives, but not me. Give me a piano and a notebook. I never needed a ball or a puck or a pair of pointe shoes. Just words and music.

"Okay, lay it on me. You didn't stop by at eight a.m. just to surprise me with coffee. Although I will love you forever for it. I swear, Lennox goes on sleep strike when Leo is gone, and Izzy was a bear to get up and dressed for school this morning. I haven't known you that long, Lilah, but I know you well enough to know something is eating at you."

Addie's hair is up in a messy bun, and her sweats look a day or two old, but somehow my friend still looks beautiful. Natural. Comfortable in her own skin. I'm not sure I remember what it's like to be comfortable in my skin. "I've known you long enough to consider you one of my best friends, Adelaide. And I don't have a whole lot of people I trust or let in."

"Don't make me cry, Lilah. It's too early for tears." She reaches out and takes my hand. "I'm so lucky to have met you. Definitely a perk of marrying Leo."

"Ha. I'm a perk. I'm so holding that over his head," I tease and give Lennox more muffin when she nips at my fingers. Pretty sure that was her way of saying, *hey lady, don't forget about me.* "I don't know, I just wanted to see you and this little girl. I wanted to talk to someone for a few minutes who wasn't going to tell me how to live my life."

"Good lord. If you could please figure out how I should live mine and let me know, I'd love you forever. I'd never dare to tell you how to live yours when I can't figure out my own. Anything I can do to help?"

I snuggle Lennox a little tighter and relax the way I swear Killian did when he held me last night. "Nope. Not unless you tell me how to deal with overbearing, overprotective men."

"Sex," she deadpans. "After an orgasm or two, I forget about how overbearing and overprotective Leo is. Well, I forget it annoys me and let it turn me on instead. Add possessive, and you've got yourself hot sex."

"Eww," I gag. "My cousin used to eat bugs. And one of the overbearing men is my brother."

Addie looks over the lid of her pink paper coffee cup at me, not convinced. "One of them may be, but you love Noah. He's not what's bothering you. There's another man bothering you. You wouldn't come here to bitch about Noah."

I sip my tea instead of answering, and she points her finger in my face. "Well, now I *know* there's someone." Her eyes light up with excitement. "Who? Is he from town or the tour? You've been holding out on me, Ryan."

Lennox grabs the muffin from my hand and tries to shove it in her mouth, and I take the distraction as a reprieve, unsure of what I want to admit to her mother . . . Or myself.

"*Y*ou've got to be kidding me," I declare with all seriousness, not finding any of this funny.

The head of my label sits across from me at the table, with my tour manager on one side and her VP of marketing on the other. She doesn't smile. Hell, she looks as pissed as I feel. "Not even a little bit, Lilah. We can't even get insurance to cover the rest of the tour. We've got to cancel the remaining eight venues and refund the tickets."

"No. I'll insure it myself before I'll do that." I refuse to let some unknown creep control my life and my career that I've worked my ass off for.

"Lilah," my manager, Scottie, blurts out. "We should discuss this."

I glance her way, then let my eyes stop briefly on my publicist, Zoe, before I turn back to Iris. No need to even look at Noah. I may be pissed at him over last night, but he's a steady, supporting force to my left. A united front, as always. "I will not cancel eight stops."

"Your safety and the safety of everyone in the venues has to come first," Iris tells me calmly, like she's rehearsed it. "Tell me you understand that."

"Don't talk to me like I'm a green newbie getting ready for her first tour, Iris. I understand safety. I also understand refusing to allow some crazy person to dictate my life and my tour. I didn't even want to do this tour in the first place, but you insisted. Now there is absolutely no way I'm going to disappoint thousands of fans and tell the world that I'm too scared to do my job all in one fell swoop. Find insurance, or I'll fund it myself." I push back from the enormous board-room table and rise with my head held as high as I can. "This is my life."

"I'll keep working on it on one condition," Iris stops me.

She waits until I give her my full attention. "You agree to increase security."

I open my mouth, but she shakes her head. "I mean it, Lilah. I need someone on you at all times. No sneaking off like you did this morning."

"What the fuck?" I look from her to Noah, but my brother shakes his head. "Xander called you?" Blood roars in my ears. Guess that means I'm firing Xander.

"Of course, he advised me. He works for me." She bristles, closing the black leather folio in front of her with a slap. "Everyone out. I want to talk to Lilah alone."

"You okay?" Scottie asks and waits for my okay before she packs up and walks out with Zoe. Noah, however, doesn't move.

"I'm sorry, Noah. Did you think that meant you could stay?" Iris snaps, and my brother doesn't even flinch.

He crosses his arms and leans back in the chair. "I'd like to see you try to move me, Iris. Anything you say to her, you can say in front of me."

"You heard him," I echo and wait.

"You two drive me absolutely fucking crazy. You know that, right?" It's not the first time she's told us that. "Fine. Like I said, if you agree to an increased security presence, I'll continue exploring insurance options. But only if you agree, Lilah. This isn't about the money. It's about your life."

"Fine. But I want them to work for me, not you. A family friend owns a security company," I argue, thinking of Maddox's dad.

"No. Hard no. Your security team works for us. Nonnegotiable."

"Nothing is nonnegotiable, Iris. If you want my security increased, I'll agree to one more man." I can't believe I'm about to say this, but I'm not sure I have a better option either. Better to deal with the devil you know. Noah squeezes my hand, and the overwhelming urge to kick him in the balls comes hard and fast. I debate it for all of thirty seconds before I hear Iris's sigh. *Fuck.* "One man." I cannot believe I'm saying this, but I've laid it down now. Might as well commit. "He can live inside my house. He can go everywhere with me. And he can basically beat anyone to death with his bare hands."

I drop Noah's hand and focus on Iris. She's got to buy into this. She has to. I don't have a better option . . . even if I know I'm going to regret it. "To the world, we'll look like a couple in love. But he'll never let anyone near me."

"And does this magical man have a name?" Intrigued, she lowers her chin and waits me out as my heart and head wage an internal battle big enough to put *Game Of Thrones* to shame.

"He's the UFC World Heavyweight Champion."

"Killian St. James," she scoffs. "You want me to put Scarlet Kingston's son in danger?"

"Scarlet St. James," I correct her.

"I don't give a flying fuck who she married. She's still Scarlet Kingston, and she's never going to agree to this," Iris argues, clearly having come across Killian's formidable mother before.

"It was Killian's idea, and he's a grown man with a mind of his own. I promise you he's in, and this won't backfire." I leave off the part where I think it won't backfire on her because this crazy scheme is absolutely going to bite me in the ass.

Iris finally sits down and opens her folio, tapping her pen as she considers what I just laid out. Eventually, a small smile creeps up on her lips. "This could work. It would be great PR for both of you, and no one would even think to step up to that mountain of a man. But you still have to let me increase your other team. They don't have to be inside your house or inside the events with you if he is, but they check it all out and stay outside the entire time."

When I open my mouth, she stops me. "No. Lilah, he's not trained for this the way they are. He can be your body man, but I want professionals checking locations. I want them driving. I want them armed. Don't fight me on this. You will not win."

"Not in my house. That's nonnegotiable." My nerves and my anger tumble with my growing frustration, along with the unbelievable hurt that mixes in whenever Killian is involved, and I have no doubt I just made a deal with the devil because there's no way I'm getting out of this unscathed.

Alive isn't the same as unhurt.

Killian

Chapter 7

*M*addox's brother, Rome, straddles heavyweight and welterweight, but he's one hell of a sparring partner no matter what weight he's sitting at. Today, we stand across from each other, waiting for my father's go, and the psychopath smiles around his black mouthguard when we get it. "With your shield—"

"Or on your shield," I finish, we tap knuckles, and I step to my right, knowing Rome is going to come at my weak left shoulder. My sparring partners don't go light on me. It doesn't do either of us any good.

The air from the missed hit flurries by my face. Rotating with fast feet, I get him with a one-two hook, nailing his jaw. The crazy fucker smiles as his head snaps back.

"Head in the game, Killer," Dad yells, and we keep going. This is fun for us. People ask all the time why we do it . . . why we put our bodies through it when there's a fifty-fifty chance you'll lose every time you step in the cage. What they don't realize is there's no fifty-fifty chance. We train harder every day than everyone else in this industry so when we step in that cage, we know without a doubt we're going to win. We don't slack off between fights. We don't go easy and get fat and lazy. We fight, take a few days to heal, and then we're back here training again. Cade St. James won't accept less. And while we might all bitch about his methods, there's no bitching about the results.

Hands up and shoulders curved, he advances.

"To the mat, Killer." Dad's voice is loud enough to drown out everything else, but somehow, I still manage to hear my name and the delicate voice it comes from just before I take a fist to the jaw and get thrown back against the cage.

Fuck.

We break apart, and I see Lilah walking over to us. There're no leggings today. She's dressed in jeans that mold to her hips like they were made to cup her ass and black patent-leather high heels, high enough to make a man think about all the things he wants to do to her with those damn shoes on. A white button-down shirt makes her look just a little bit like a naughty librarian and definitely looks sexier than it should, which makes my brain hurt and my dick hard.

"Goddamn, Lilah Ryan would look so pretty on her knees," Rome whispers, and I swing my fist with no finesse and knock him out.

Oops.

"Killer—" Dad yells as Lilah steps up to the mat, careful not to step on it in her shoes.

Good girl.

She remembers.

"Sorry." I spit my mouthguard out. "I need a few minutes."

I don't wait to get my ass chewed out, even though I know it's coming. And that shit's definitely coming.

"Hi, Mr. St. James. It's good to see you," she says sweetly.

He takes in where she stands and the respect she just showed by not walking on the mats in her fancy red-soled shoes and groans. "Ten minutes, Killian. Don't keep him longer than that, Lilah."

"I won't." She smiles her sweetest smile, and Dad melts. Lilah has that effect on people. She always has.

I press my hand against the small of her back and urge her forward.

She goes with it but steels her spine under my touch. "Where are you taking me?"

"Brynlee's office. She's not here right now." We move into the back of the gym and step inside one of the few rooms in this building that has a door.

"Wow . . . Your dad expanded," she whispers, and pride swells in my chest. This place has been in my family for two generations. I was raised here, and I want to raise my own kids here . . . one day.

"Yeah. Everyone wants to be trained by the best, and Dad and Hudson are the best." I close the door and watch her examining the pictures framed on Brynlee's wall. She's buying time. She wants to talk but not until she's ready. There's never been any rushing Lilah. She doesn't play that way. "You doing okay, princess?"

"I hate that nickname." The words don't have the same strength they did the last time I saw her.

"No, you don't," I say more gently than last night. "Why are you here, Lilah?"

Her shoulders rise and fall with a deep inhale, and giant diamond stud earrings glint under the harsh fluorescent light when she finally spins around. "Would you believe me if I said I don't know?"

Her eyes are so blue you'd think contacts made them that color, but they're all her.

They get darker when she cries, but she never lets anyone see that.

At least she didn't used to.

Long, black lashes kiss her cheeks as she closes her eyes, seemingly gathering her strength. Every muscle in my body contracts. This girl is about to ask me for something, it's written in every tightly held line of her body, and she hasn't asked me for anything in so damn long.

"Did you mean what you said last night?" Her voice is barely above a whisper, and it kills me to hear it like that. Hear *her* like that.

"Every fucking word."

She paces Brynlee's office like a wild animal, desperate to break its confines. "This doesn't change anything. I still hate you, St. James."

Those words sting as much today as they did a decade ago, but this clusterfuck of a situation might finally be my chance to right a fucking wrong and fix it all. "You never hated me, princess, and this changes everything."

A million emotions flash across her beautiful face before she settles on a sad smile I can't stand to see. "You broke me once, Killian. I won't let you do that again."

"Then why trust me with this?" I step up into her space, tired of this bullshit dance we're dancing and take her hand in mine. "Why come to me if you hate me as much as you claim to?" When she doesn't answer, I close the distance between us. "Because I don't think you ever really hated me. You hated yourself. You hated what happened. And yeah, you hated my part in it. But I'm gonna bet you never hated me. And now, I'm the only one who can protect you. Karma's a bitch, princess."

Fire erupts in her cheeks, and her eyes glitter with anger.

Mission accomplished.

I can handle pissed-off Lilah. Broken Lilah isn't an option.

"But here's the thing . . ." I take my life in my hands and cup her face, praying she doesn't kick me in the balls. "Deep down, you know no one in this world will keep you as safe as I will. Some things don't change, no matter how many years and how big a distance. And that will never change. That's why you're standing here."

She gently pulls my hands away from her face. "I'm standing here because if I didn't agree to increased security, they weren't going to let me finish my tour, and I refuse to tell tens of thousands of fans that I'm canceling the rest of the stops on my tour. I'm not letting someone else dictate my career when I've been the one busting my ass for it for ten years. I'm standing here because you offered, and I'd rather deal with the devil I know. So I guess I need to know if you were serious last night."

"As a heart attack," I snap. No second-guessing. No fear. No question.

She nods and turns away from me, and the loss of contact shouldn't feel like this. It's not even physical contact. It's the loss of her gaze on me that feels fucking cold.

"Do you think you could spend a few nights at my place? It's just . . . Noah moved back into his own place today. *Mainly because I forced him . . .*" she mumbles the last sentence under her breath. "And the label agreed to you, if you stay close. I told them you were the only one I wanted inside my house."

Knowing that shouldn't make me feel like a fucking king.

But it does.

I move behind her, careful not to touch. "I'll be there tonight after training."

"Killian—" She spins and bounces right against my chest. Her hands press against my abs, and my hands steady her shoulders. "Why would you do this? What's in it for you?"

Fuck, she's so pretty when she forgets she hates me.

She's pretty damn gorgeous when she remembers it too.

Fuck.

"Because it's you. I'd do anything for you, Lilah." Always would. Some things you know deep in your soul won't ever change. Loving Lilah Ryan in one way or another was never going to change for me. Maybe this is my chance to change it for her . . . Maybe.

"Not anything, champ." She reaches her hand up like she's going to touch my face but drops it instead. "My assistant set up a meal service for me. If you text me what you like to eat, I'll make sure we're stocked."

"I'm in training—"

"Chicken and brown rice?" she asks, and I nod. "Broccoli? Salmon? Protein shakes?"

"Yeah . . ." Fuck . . . she remembers.

"Okay. I guess I'll see you tonight. We can talk about everything then." Lilah steps around me. "Please apologize to your dad for me. I didn't mean to interrupt your training."

I shrug, and she smiles. "I mean, it looked like Rome was kicking your ass, so maybe I was helping you."

"Rome wasn't winning, princess." Fuck that. She saw one move. One distraction *that she caused.*

"Whatever you've gotta tell yourself to sleep at night, St. James. I'll make sure Noah's bed has clean sheets to lie to yourself in." She giggles as she opens the door.

"Already worried about where I'm going to be sleeping, huh? Should I be worried about my virtue?" I tease her. This is where we find common ground. Always did.

"Your virtue was shredded years ago, Killian. Try not to take mine with it, okay? I've got a brand to live up to." She wiggles her fingers and pulls the door closed behind her.

Her virtue is still . . . intact?

What the hell does that mean, and why am I ravenous to find out for myself?

Lilah

Chapter 8

I saw somewhere that butterflies rest when it rains because it damages their wings. It was supposed to remind you it's okay to rest during the storms in life because you'll fly again when it's over. Here's the thing . . . I think there's something wrong with me because I don't want to be the butterfly. I want to be the storm. I'll rest when I'm dead.

—Lilah's Secret Thoughts

"**M**om?" I stare, my mouth agape when I open my door to Mom and Dillan, both standing on my front steps, grocery bags in one hand and a bottle of wine in the other. "What are you doing here?"

"Lilah Belle Ryan . . ." Mom leans in and kisses my cheek, then hip-checks me. "Step aside."

Shit. It's never good when you get full-named in my family.

"Whatever you say." I push open the door and wait for her to walk by before I hold Dillan back. "Why does she look like she's up to something?"

"Because she is," Dillan squeaks and ducks past, then spins around to face me as she walks backward through my foyer. "But she brought strawberries, vanilla bean ice cream, and chocolate fudge with her. So maybe don't piss her off until after I've had some, okay?"

I can feel the headache coming on already.

Like this day hasn't been long enough.

Dillan spins back around again and follows Mom down the hall, with me trailing behind her. *In my own house.* Ugh.

Guess we're going to the kitchen.

"Honey . . ." Mom looks up when Dillan and I walk in. "Where is your bottle opener?"

"Umm . . ." I move over to the drawer I think I saw it in the other day and rummage around until I find it. "What are you doing here, Mom?"

She takes the fancy-shmancey opener out of my hand and points at me with it. "I'm soaking up quality time with my girls. Is that a crime?"

Deep breath in . . . slow breath out.

Do not lose your shit on your mother.

"No, Mom. It's just been a long day, and I didn't know you were coming." I pull out a chair at the island and plant my ass, preparing myself for whatever is about to come. Because something is certainly coming. My mother is nothing if not crazy. Amazing. Loving. Possibly the best mother in the world. But she's as crazy as anyone I've ever met.

She collects three stemless wine glasses from the glass-front cabinet and cracks open a bottle of rosé. "Oh, Lilah . . . We never got any time during the holidays for just the three of us. I felt like we were overdue for a girls' night."

I look over at the clock and that quick movement doesn't escape her. "Are we keeping you from something?"

Dillan pushes a glass my way, then takes one for herself. "Oh, this ought to be good," she giggles, and I glare.

"What the fuck?" I murmur.

"Language," Mom chides.

Dillan chokes on her wine. "Oh please, Mom. We learned to curse from you."

I nod. "True. Daddy used to watch what he was saying in front of us."

"Whatever. Your father curses worse than I do. What were you *what the fucking*? Or should I ask who?" Now, this is probably what she's really here for. Damn this town. Gossip travels faster than the speed of light around here.

"I'm not fucking anyone," I tell them both and sip my wine. "And if you want to go down this road, you better hand me a spoon because I'm gonna need some ice cream."

Mom pulls a carton of bright red strawberries from her bag and shakes them in front of me. "Where's your cutting board, Tink?"

I motion to the left of the sink and sit back as she goes to work on the strawberries, praying that's the last of the *who's Lilah banging* conversation but knowing it's not.

"Okay . . ." Dillan snags a berry from Mom and pops it in her mouth. "So . . . going back to you *what the fucking . . .*"

I growl at my little sister. Legit growl.

"Yes," Mom exclaims. "I heard a rumor today—"

"There it is," I announce.

"What?" My beautiful mother looks around, trying to appear as innocent as possible.

Newsflash.

She's the farthest thing from innocent.

"Oh please, Mom. The smile on your face when you walked through my door meant you were up to something. I just had to figure out what it was. And now I know. So . . . let me be proactive here. I am not *what the fucking* anyone. I haven't been for a long . . . long . . . long time." I turn my eyes on my sister. "Now you, on the other hand. I may have heard a rumor or two too."

The next strawberry she picks up gets thrown at my head.

"Really?" Mom turns to grab bowls, but Dillan and I go right for the spoons and the ice cream instead.

"Where's the fudge?" I ask her and smile deliciously when Dillan grabs it from the bag and drizzles it right over the carton of ice cream as I reach across the island with my spoon and drag the strawberries closer. The two of us tap spoons like we used to when we were kids and dig in before Mom even turns around.

"Oh . . . Okay." She picks up her own spoon and leans across the island to get a spoonful too. "Okay. You." She points toward Dillan. "You're on deck. I want to know what your sister is talking about with you too. But you first." She swallows her scoop of ice cream and moans—actually moans—then points at me.

"Mom, please." Good lord. How are we not all more fucked up than we are?

"Sorry. Okay, focused. We heard a rumor today, and I'm going to need you to clear it up."

I look over at Dillan, like she might be able to telepathically tell me what the hell Mom heard, even if I've got a pretty good idea. But you never know. And I don't really want to give her the Killian scoop if that's not what she's talking about. I've got to tread carefully.

"Noah and I had the meeting with the label this morning." I drag another spoonful through the fudge, then dip it in the bowl of berries, hoping my mouthful will give her a minute to answer.

It doesn't work.

Mom and Dillan wait me out.

Is it better to get it over with and just tell them?

Maybe I'll test the waters.

"I think it went okay. Not the best but not the worst either." There. That wasn't too painful.

"Did it really end with you in an arranged marriage to one of the hottest men in Kroydon Hills?" Dillan reaches out for more ice cream, but I slap her hand away with my spoon.

"Are you insane? Like actually out of your mind?" I pull the entire carton of vanilla bean goodness my way and refuse to share. "You don't actually believe that. Come on . . ."

Her evil smile grows like the Cheshire fucking cat.

"Believe it? No. Did I hear it . . . ? I may have," she admits, and as I sit there with my mouth gaping open, she takes it as her opening to steal the ice cream back.

Twat.

"From who?" I'm aware my voice just increased to a frighteningly high decibel.

Oh well.

She blinks, like she can't believe I managed that sound, before schooling her face. "I cannot divulge my sources."

"Ugh." I flick her forehead, and she tries to shove me back but misses. "Mom."

"Sorry, Tink. That's what I heard too. Well, sort of."

I swear sometimes when I look at my mother, I feel like I'm looking at my reflection in twenty years, and it makes me so happy. She's beautiful and kind and awesome . . . and I'm gonna kill her. "You two are such bullshitters."

My mother sips her wine and pulls herself up to sit on the counter. "But it's so much fun, honey."

"I hate you," I groan, but at least I do it with a smile.

"No, you don't," they both chime back.

"Fine. Yes. I agreed to let Killian act as an additional bodyguard." Even saying the words makes me feel so incredibly pathetic. I've worked my whole life for this career. Sang my first time in front of a crowd when I was five years old. Twenty years ago. And this is what I've been reduced to.

"And he's going to be acting like your boyfriend too? Are you going to be sharing a bed?" Mom asks, and for a hot second, I wish she was an accountant instead of a world-famous romance author with two different shows running on Netflix and a movie in post-production.

"No, Mom. This isn't an only-one-bed romance." Of course, the little pang in my chest when I think of sharing a bed with Killian pisses me off almost as much as it turns me on.

No. Nope. Not happening.

Uh-uh.

It pisses me off more than it turns me on.

"Damn, Tink. That man looks so fucking hot when he's sparring. And he's so much bigger than you. Like holy size kink, batman. I'd let him do anything he wanted to me. The more depraved, the better."

Mom and I both stare at Dillan, shocked.

"Dillan Laine Ryan—" Mom finally gasps, and Dillan just shrugs and smiles.

"Seriously, Mom. His muscles have muscles. You just know he'd be—"

"Stop. Please, God, stop." I shove my spoonful of ice cream in her mouth, and she coughs. Oh well. Definitely the lesser of two evils because if my little sister keeps talking about Killian like that, I might just come up with a less tasty way to shut her up.

I may not want the man, but there was a time . . . Nope. Not thinking about that.

The little brat swallows the spoonful, then smiles so big, her dimples show.

She licks her lips and runs her finger over the corner of her mouth. "I see how it is."

"Girls," Mom warns. "Be nice and use your words. Wait . . . actually, Dillan. Maybe you should use less words.

There are some things even I don't want to know." I'd say *poor Mom* as she stands there cringing, but it serves her right.

"Yeah well, it worked." The little twat-waffle looks triumphantly between us.

"What worked?" My body tenses, feeling like somehow I just got tricked into something, but I'm not sure what.

"You, big sister, just told me what I needed to know."

Oh, I so know I'm going to regret this. "And what exactly was that?"

"Killian St. James might be playing the part of bodyguard and boyfriend, but there's enough truth buried in the lie to make it dangerous. Be careful. He's supposed to keep you safe, but it sounds like he could be more dangerous than you realize."

"Dangerous to your heart," Mom adds, and I can't help but think the romance author in her has read too many of her own books.

But the truth is they're not wrong.

He may be the biggest danger I'll ever face, because he almost broke me once.

The young girl who loved love and hearts and flowers—the one who grew up watching the best fairytale play out in front of her every day as I got to watch the way my parents loved each other—that same girl died a little when I left Kroydon Hills, and it took years to find her again. The truth is I'm not sure I ever got her back completely, and I'm not sure my heart or my head could bear going through that again.

Maybe this was a really bad idea.

I look down, suddenly very interested in counting the seeds on my strawberry.

"But here's the thing, Tink." My mom walks around the counter and lifts my face. "You are one of the strongest people I've ever known." She pushes my hair away from my face, pride emanating from every inch of her body. "I want you to hear that again because I didn't say women, I said people. Men and women. I've met all kinds in my life and you, my beautiful girl, are stronger than all of them. You have been your entire life. I know Killian was special to you when you were younger. Your father and I worried about how much time you were spending with him and the boys, but even then, you never let those relationships stop you. You still pursued your music. If anything, you were stronger *because* of them, not *in spite* of them. Those boys were your biggest fans, including Killian. Life has a way of working itself out. Maybe this is your chance to find that friendship again."

I shove the emotion back down my throat, refusing to give voice to Mom's beautiful words. "This was the only way to get the label to keep looking for insurance for the remainder of the tour."

Mom's slow nod leaves little doubt about how much she believes that, but she lets me have my lie. "If your label can't find insurance, Daddy and I talked about it after Noah left today. We'll cover it."

"Mom—"

"I love you, Lilah Belle." She tilts my head forward and kisses my forehead.

I close my eyes, refusing to let my tears fall.

"I love you too, Mom."

The Philly Press

POP PRINCESS

Rumor has it that America's favorite pop princess, Lilah Ryan, has been spotted multiple times at a certain MMA gym in town. Could it be Ms. Ryan has decided to switch careers or maybe she's human like the rest of us and is having a hard time losing the holiday weight she put on . . . ? Guess it's time to get a gym membership.

#KroydonKronicles #NewYearsResolutionUnlocked #PopPrincess

Killian

Chapter 9

"Killer—" Dad's voice carries as I walk by his office at the end of the day.

Shit. So much for making my escape.

That's about right. It's not like he didn't ride my ass after Lilah left, like I was a rookie who needed to be put through my paces.

I shoulder my gym bag, lean against his doorframe, and wait. It's coming.

Dad rests his elbows on his desk and runs his hand through his salt-and-pepper hair, much the same way I do. Guess I get it from him. Mom would say he needs a haircut, and she'd be right. She's always on the two of us about that shit. Never my sisters. She's on them for a whole mess of other stuff though, so I'll take the ribbing about my hair.

Worry lines his face, so I know I'm in for it before he opens his mouth. "We're nine weeks out from your fight, and I don't know where your head's at, kid."

I want to tell him that makes two of us, but I don't feel like dealing with the fallout from that kind of war cry, and that's exactly what it would be. One of the things that makes Cade St. James the greatest coach the league has ever seen is his ability to cut through the shit and keep his fighters focused on the only thing that matters in this sport. Winning.

"It was one day, Dad. One conversation. One fifteen-minute break," I argue, trying to set his mind at ease, even though I'm full of shit. Problem is, he knows it.

"Don't do this, Killer. Don't fucking rebel now. You know what you need to do. Don't make me say it."

No distractions. That's what he'd say, and Lilah strutting her way back into town is the biggest possible distraction imaginable. Even more than he knows.

"Not rebelling, old man." I push off the door and shift my bag. "It's good. We're good. My head's in this thing. My heart's in it too. I'm going to wipe the mat with him. That belt is going to stay mine. And you have my permission to kick my ass if I slack off at all. Sound good?"

You've got to be a cocky bastard to do what I do for a living.

Confidence is 50 percent of the battle, and I've got it in spades.

I got my first judo gi at two years old.

Fought in my first tournament at five.

Won my first state wrestling championship at eight.

I could have gone to the University of Iowa to wrestle in college if I wanted to, but I didn't. I wanted to be here in Kroydon Hills. I wanted Dad and Hudson to train me. I wanted to spar with my cousins. I wanted to be part of the next generation of fighters representing Crucible. I've got no fucking clue what's going to happen in a few years when I stop competing, but I'll figure it out when I have to. For now, this is what I want.

Dad stands and moves around his desk. He knocks his fist gently against my heart. "Make sure your heart stays in it, kid. Because you can't afford to lose it to something else for nine more weeks. Distractions are weaknesses, Killer. You know that. This fight is a year in the making. Don't lose it before you step foot in the cage."

"Locked-in. I got this." I step away, knowing I'm going to be walking a tightrope for a few weeks, but Lilah's safety is worth the walk.

Besides, I've got fucking awesome balance.

An hour later, I'm showered, packed, and standing in front of Lilah's front door with my fist raised to knock when I come face-to-face with a giggling Dillan. "Fighter boy." She points her finger at my chest, then leans in and taps me. "You came. Good boy." Another tap. "Don't let anything happen to my sister, and maybe try protecting your pretty face while you're at it. You're fun to look at, but that bruise . . ." Her finger moves up to my jaw, and she presses the bruise where Rome got me with his knee.

"Dillan—stop molesting Killian." Nattie Ryan walks outside, her keys in her hand as she remotely starts her car, shaking her head. "God grant me the patience to deal with my headstrong daughters." She pulls Dillan's hand away from me and pats her like she's a little kid. "Go wait for me in the car, sweets."

"But—" The argument dies on the younger Ryan's lips with one look at her mother. "Fine."

"Sorry about Dillan. I may have filled her wine glass a few too many times." Nattie Ryan is a gorgeous woman and looks more like she could be Lilah's older sister than her mother. Her long golden hair and tiny frame remind me so much of her daughter, but the look in her eyes tells me she's about to call me out on something. It's the same look Lilah gets, only her daughter hasn't given a shit what I've done for a decade. "What are you doing here, Killian? Don't think I don't know you and Lilah haven't been friends for a long time."

Christ. How many people are going to call me out tonight?

My dad, Dillan, and now Nattie Ryan.

Is my mom going to show up next?

"I'm here to help an old friend out. That's it," I try to rationalize, but even to me, it sounds like bullshit.

"Uh-huh. An old friend." She looks at the bag in my hand. "You pack a bag to see all your old friends?"

I don't bother answering. She already knows the answer.

"Yeah . . . didn't think so. Listen, Killian. You're a good kid—"

Jesus. How many fucking people are going to call me a kid tonight?

"You always were. Brady and I knew the way Jamie, Maverick, and you watched out for Lilah in high school. You boys were so sweet. But you're not in high school. Actions have consequences . . ." She takes a beat, straightens her back, and rests her hand on my shoulder. "Just tread lightly, okay? My girl is going through hell right now."

The tiny woman looks heartbroken at the thought of Lilah hurting, but she shakes it away. Lilah Ryan would kick her mother's ass from here to Philadelphia if she knew she was saying any of this to me, and Nattie knows it. "I'm sure I'll see you again soon. Hopefully, before the twins' birthday." She squeezes my shoulder and drops her hand. "'Night."

"'Night, Mrs. Ryan," I murmur, stuck in the past, remembering the way Lilah used to love Noah's and her birthday. Of course, the girl who used to love *love* and hearts and flowers and romance would be born on Valentine's Day. The five of us always used to do something special and usually stupid, like sneaking out after curfew and getting up to something we shouldn't have been doing. But Lilah's hand

BELLA MATTHEWS

was always in mine when we did whatever the hell we thought was cool that year.

The year she left for her first tour, her birthday was one of the last fun days we had.

Fuck.

I hadn't thought about that in so damn long.

"Killian . . ." Her voice shakes me from the memory. The good and the bad parts of it. "I didn't know you were here."

I watch her Mom pull out of Lilah's driveway and shrug. "Sorry. I was talking to your mom and sister. Did you know your gate was open?"

She looks at the black, wrought-iron gate in the far distance at the end of her driveway and shakes her head. "No. I didn't. Mom must have left it open when she came in."

"How many people have access to get in?" I push as she guides me inside and purses her lips.

"Just my immediate family. They're the only ones with the code. Them and my security team . . . well, and I guess now you. You'll need it." Her bright blue eyes rake over my bag. "I know we talked about you spending the night, but you don't have to. I mean—ugh. This is so frustrating. It's just, I mean . . . Well, you don't have to sleep here. You can go home. We could work something else out."

Her creamy skin heats and pinks as she grows more and more flustered.

"Sorry, princess, but when I agreed to this, I told you I'm all-in. Where you go, I go. Where you sleep—"

"Down the hall," she cuts me off. "You are not sleeping in my room."

"I don't have to sleep in your room, Lilah. But I'm sleeping in your house . . ." I trail off, not wanting to piss her off on my first night here. I've had a lot of time to think about us and our fucked up relationship while I sat in the steam room today, and I decided something. This is my opportunity to fix our shitty past. If she's going to be stuck with me, she's going to have to listen, *eventually*.

"*Killian . . .*" she pouts, like we're still sixteen, and that pout will get her whatever she wants.

"Not a chance, Lilah." I drop my bag on the floor and stuff my hands in the front pocket of my Crucible hoodie. "I think it's time we establish some ground rules."

Her mouth opens and closes a few times, like that beta fish I won her at the carnival when we were thirteen. "Ground rules?"

"Yup." I pull out one of her island stools and leave my hand on the back. "Sit."

"I'm not a dog, St. James." The venom is back, but I'll take that over the woman who struggled to get her words out a minute ago. Lilah is cool, calm, and confident. She always has been, and it fucking hurts to see her anything less.

"Nope. More like stubborn like a damn mule, Ryan." I screech the stool against the floor and push it behind her until she has no choice but to climb up and sit her fine ass down. "Now let's hammer this out."

"If I had a hammer, I'd hit you over the head with it," she snaps back with a haughty tone in her voice that shouldn't be hot, but it is.

I move around the stool and rest my ass against the counter in front of her. "Where you go, I go, and I have to go to Crucible five days a week to train."

"I train too, but I'm not staying there all day. Xander can bring me home when I'm done," she argues.

"You gonna let him inside the house?" I question, not liking how dismissive she sounds about her safety.

"No. You are the only non-friend or family I'm letting into my home. Rule number one. You don't bring anyone here."

"I wouldn't, and you know it." I focus on the annoyance

that she felt like she even had to say that shit instead of the fact that she doesn't consider me a friend. I knew it, but it still sucks to hear it. Damn, this is gonna be harder than I thought. "If I'm not with you, you gotta let Lurch stick by your side if you're outside the house. Don't fuck with your safety, Lilah."

"Don't call him Lurch," she groans. "I'm gonna kill Dillan."

"For more reasons than that nickname," I mumble. "And if we're supposed to pull off the whole couple vibe, you're going to have to act like you can stand me."

"In public," she grits through her teeth. "I'm a performer. I can manage. The question is can you? But then again, you're the better liar of the two of us."

"Fuck, Lilah. I'll do this for you, but you've got to give it a break. We both fucked up back then. We were kids. We're not the same people." Any man who tries to say words can't hurt never had Lilah Ryan tell him she hates him. It fucking sucks.

"Fine. We'll probably need to make a few public appearances to really sell this." She reaches up and twists her long blonde curls into a knot on top of her head, then slaps her hands down on her thighs, dragging my eyes down to the hot-pink leggings molded to her perfectly shaped thighs. Thighs that would looks so fucking good straddling my face.

And now I'm smiling, and if she knew why, she'd kick my ass. It would serve me right too.

"Do you want to go to the Superbowl this weekend? My family has a suite," I offer, and this little brat rolls her eyes.

"Yeah, champ, so does mine. One of my uncles coaches the team, and the other plays for them, remember? I can go without you if I want to." Her haughty voice comes right back into play, and my cock jerks in response. "But no, I don't want to go. I'd rather not do anything quite that high-profile."

This shit is going to be harder than I thought.

Pretty goddamn sure I'm going to be harder than I thought too. I see a lot of cold fucking showers in my future.

"No need to argue, princess. My family owns the team, and yours runs it. I get it. Okay, we'll skip the game. I've got a Kingston charity event at the beginning of March. We can go to that."

"Whatever. I'm sure someone will get a picture of us coming and going from Crucible. It'll get out. Trust in the paparazzi. They always find a way. I'm surprised the *Kroydon Kronicles* hasn't published anything about me at your gym. Looks like their bite has gotten less brutal."

"Haven't seen their post today, have you?" I hate that the color drains from her face. "Ignore it. Like you said, they were going to see us there together at some point. And if not, they're going to see you at my fight."

She runs her fingers around a red-braided bracelet tied around her wrist in a safety blanket kind of way. "You want me to come to your fight? It's the championship fight, right?" she whispers, and something about her voice is like a punch to the jaw that nearly drops me. It's the hesitance mixed with something else. Hope, maybe . . . ?

I wrap my hand around her neck, feeling a little less like I'm risking life and limb this time, but she still bristles and tenses. "Yeah, princess. I'm defending my title."

"I guess it's the least I can do to repay the favor you're doing for me. After all, I can cheer for the guy beating your ass." She lifts a perfectly arched eyebrow, and her blue eyes sparkle.

"Brat," I laugh. "I don't get beat."

"A girl can only hope," she singsongs with a sly smile, until I squeeze just a touch against her neck, and the smile turns into something else. Something hotter. "Kidding . . . I was kidding. I may not like you very much, but I spent enough time watching you train that I want you to win, St. James. I may hope the guy gets in a good hit or two to knock your pretty face around a bit, but I want you to win."

She hops down off the stool and away from my touch. "Terms accepted. Now I'm going to bed." She grabs a bottle of water from the fridge and stops in front of me. "Alone. You can have the room Noah slept in. It's not like it's the first time you had his sloppy seconds."

Touché, princess . . . touché.

"I'll set the alarm code and text that and the gate code to you. Your room is the third room on the right at the top of the stairs, and mine is the one next to it."

"Sweet dreams, princess."

"More like nightmares, champ. See you in the morning."

I'm so stuck on that word—nightmares—that I almost miss the way her heart-shaped ass sways as she walks away. Almost. I might be a nice guy, but I'm only human, and Lilah Ryan is the perfect woman wrapped up in a tight, hot, little package. She's gonna be the death of me. Let's just hope not literally.

Lilah

Chapter 10

Expecting me to be the bigger person when I'm 5'2" is where you made your first mistake. I'm tiny. That just means I learned early on how to kick when I fight back.

—Lilah's Secret Thoughts

"You have a gym in your basement." It's not a question, but the irritating way Killian barks the words at me feels like a question wrapped in an accusation.

I pull my favorite chunky knit blanket tighter around my shoulders and lay my notebook down on the couch before I even bother turning to look at him.

It's way too early for this shit. The sun has barely risen. This is my quiet time. When the world is still asleep and my thoughts are more clear than any other time of day. I haven't looked at social media. Haven't checked my emails or my messages. Haven't usually talked to another human being. It's my favorite time to write. And that voice just stole my peace.

"It's not even six-thirty yet, St. James. Why are you awake?" I turn my head and come face-to-face with Killian,

83

who's moved and is now leaning behind me, his fists clutching the back of the couch. It's more like face-to-chest . . . And holy fucking ab muscles.

Did they get bigger since I saw him in the cage yesterday? I mean . . . there's eight of them. Big and defined and kinda bulging right in front of my eyes.

Dillan would love being this up close and personal with those muscles. She'd climb him like a tree. A sturdy tree, strong enough to hold her steady. Stupid fucking tree.

My eyes track a tiny bead of sweat as it trickles down over his abs like it's running over a literal washboard. I really shouldn't want to lick that bead of sweat.

Shouldn't. Not don't.

Stupid, *stupid* man and his stupidly godlike body.

Seriously . . . what did I do wrong in a different life that he's the only person I could go to for help? The one person I can trust to do it, even if it's the only thing I can trust him with? I mean, this is just not fair.

"Hey, princess . . ." He snaps his fingers in front of my face, and I smack them away. "My eyes are up here."

I arch a brow and purse my lips in an attempt to look unimpressed.

Doubt it works.

"Keep dreaming, St. James." Why the hell is it so hot in here?

"I get up at five a.m. every day to get my run in if I can before I go to Crucible. Why are you up?"

I tuck my legs under the blanket and turn away from him. "It's easier to write when the world around me is quiet."

Killian's green eyes narrow, like he wants to know more, but he's smart enough not to push, so I change the topic and answer his earlier question, "Of course I have a home gym. I thought I mentioned that. When I had the house built, I made sure to have the basement fitted for a gym on one side and a soundproof recording studio on the other. I want to be able to do as much here as possible."

"Sounds like you're hiding, Lilah." He tugs my arm so I'm forced to bend my neck and look at him. I should hate the move. Mostly because it's what he used to do whenever he wanted my attention. And of course it still works. *Asshole.*

"I'm not hiding. I just like the quiet." I can hear the lie in my own words as easily as he probably can. "Don't you ever get tired of the noise? You've got to have a ton of it in your world too. Especially with a fight coming up. I bet everyone wants a piece of you."

Killian wraps my hair around his finger and plays with the curl.

It would be so easy to close my eyes and pretend . . .

Act like the past ten years didn't happen.

That we weren't completely different people now than we were then.

But I don't. I can't.

There's no going backward in life if you want to be sure of what's in front of you.

"Come on now . . . you know my Dad would rip me out of his cage by my balls if I let the noise in. Easiest way to lose a fight is to fight distracted. One of the first things we learn to do is tune it all out." He tugs again, then drops my hair. "So what time can you be ready to head to Crucible?"

"What?" I spin around to face him and get caught in my blanket like a turtle caught in his own shell, yanking my legs and arms free but getting more tangled before I can finally rip it off. I lift up on my knees and grab the back of the couch so I'm closer to his height. Well, not really, but at least I'm a little higher. "Did you not just hear me say I have everything set up so I can chill and write and regroup in the privacy and quiet of my own home?"

Killian slides his hands up my ribs and under my arms

and lifts me from the couch and plants my feet on the floor like I'm a rag doll he can move at will.

"No—" I snap and smack away his hands. "You cannot just move me because you feel like it, you jerk."

He crosses his thick freaking arms over his chest and glares. "You asked me why I was up? Well I'm training for my next title fight, princess. I've got to defend my title against some asshole who's hungry as hell for my belt, and that means I've got to train harder than him. That starts before I set foot in the gym, and it doesn't end when I get home at night. If you need me by your side, I'm gonna need you at Crucible."

Jesus. Can't he at least put a shirt on if he's going to lecture me?

It would make it easier to focus on his words instead of his muscles.

I reach over and grab my notebook from the couch in a huff. "Fine. But I'm not staying there all day."

"Then I guess you're letting Xander inside, aren't you? Because you need to have someone with you at all times, Lilah. If you're home, maybe you can get away with one of the other guys. Jamie or Noah or Maddox or Rome. Hell, Maverick's season will be over after this weekend. He can bring Rosie over with him.

"That's not fair," I mumble. Rosie is the sweetest little girl in the world, and Maverick is so protective of who he lets around her that Killian knows how much we all dote on her. "Don't use Rosie against me."

"I'll use every weapon in my arsenal if I have to. Now go get dressed. If I'm late today, I'll never hear the end of it."

The way his eyes are cast down over me, I know he's daring me to argue, and I refuse to give him what he wants.

He's doing me a favor.

I have to be nice . . . right?

It's a shame nice goes right out the window where this man is concerned, and slightly irrational anger replaces it with the heat of a billion burning suns.

Maybe one day, I'll release my negativity into the universe, but today is not that day.

Today, I'm holding on to it like a safety blanket.

"Fine. I'll go with you this morning and ask Xander if he can bring me home later so I can get some work done too." I clutch my notebook to my chest. It's not like I haven't spent a few hours a day at the gym for the past week anyway. "Do you guys have any good classes I could take?"

His green eyes twinkle as we walk side by side out of the room. "What kind of classes?"

"High-intensity? Something that's going to work everything? I'm trying to lose a few inches." My skin itches with the thought of that damn article and the way they compared the photos of me from two years ago to my photos now. Nothing like seeing yourself side by side to see every pound you've gained.

Killian slams his hand against the door frame, nearly clotheslining me before I can make my escape.

"What the hell, St. James?" I squeak and duck under his arm. "You're supposed to be keeping me safe, not nearly knocking me out."

"Lilah, stop." His voice . . . that voice . . . It's gravelly. Strong but quiet. So damn serious, it sends chills down my arms. "Please."

The *please* stops me in my tracks, but I don't turn around. I can't. I'm frozen in place, certain I don't want to look into his eyes right now. I know it in the depths of my soul.

Damn him.

"Don't listen to them, princess. Don't let them in your head. You, Lilah Belle Ryan, are fucking perfect. You're beautiful, and you're kind . . . well, to everyone who isn't me. So what if you gained a pound or two, Lilah. They look really fucking good on you."

Goosebumps break out over my skin when his voice is suddenly closer, and his breath skirts over my skin.

"Your curves are perfect." His words are slow and heavy and make my knees weaker than they should. Weaker than I'll ever admit. "Your legs are the kind men fantasize about getting lost between for fucking days."

Killian's breathing slows and grows heavy, like he's forcing himself to regulate it. Like he's holding on to an invisible string, refusing to allow it to snap.

The energy in the room shifts.

It thickens.

Like it has its own pulse. Its own heartbeat.

"If you were mine, I'd worship every inch of your body every day." I can feel his hand reach out, like he's going to touch me, but he doesn't, and suddenly I'm not sure whether I'm disappointed or relieved. "I'd make damn sure you knew how much I appreciated every . . . incredible . . . curve."

His hand flutters by me as he drops it and angles toward me long enough to see his eyes harden and narrow before he storms off, leaving me standing here, completely shaken.

Oh. My. God.

What the hell was that?

Killian

"Killer," Hudson calls out as I work the battle ropes in the corner of the room, fucking desperate for something mindless. I need something that's gonna make me so goddamn tired, I'll forget the line I already came dangerously close to crossing.

The first of how many mornings I have to wake up and smell Lilah Ryan?

Sugar and a sweet spice . . . vanilla maybe. Like a Belgium waffle.

Sweet and spicy. Perfect for her.

I'm so screwed.

"Killian—" Hudson grabs the rope, stopping the motion. Stopping me. "What the fuck, kid? Where the hell are you? I've been trying to talk to you for ten minutes."

I stare at my uncle, one-half of my training team, and wait for him to drop the rope, already so on edge I don't want to talk.

Not to him. Not to anyone.

"I'm sorry. Did you think that was a rhetorical fucking question? When I speak, you answer or you get the hell off the mats."

Hudson Kingston, my mom's younger brother, my dad's first fighter to win a belt training under him, and in some ways my uncle, but in others, the older brother I never had. He's rarely a hard-ass, so when he is, I know it's bad.

"Do I need to change into red booty shorts and a tight white tank to get your attention or are my tits just not quite big enough for you?"

I drop the rope, plant one foot, and knock all six and a half feet, two hundred and forty pounds of him back five feet with the other, driving us both down to the mat. He lands with a bounce like I knew he would, this mat has springs under it, and I straddle his waist. "Watch your fucking mouth, Uncle."

"Woo-hoo," he blows out and shakes his head. "It's like that already, huh?"

He doesn't try to fight me.

He could try to flip us to get me out of the mount and into a position he can control, but he doesn't. He doesn't even try.

"Kid, you're so fucking screwed, you don't even know it yet."

I release my hold and drop back on the mat. "Yeah, I actually do, *thanks*."

Lilah isn't even fifteen feet away from me, walking on the damn StairMaster again. Like her ass isn't already enough to bring a man to his knees. Worse, that thought makes me want to kill any motherfucker who looks her way.

"I'm well aware of exactly how screwed I am, thanks," I groan.

"Your mom and dad know, you know?" Hudson sits up and offers me his hand.

I take his hand and let him pull me to my feet. "You talking in riddles for a reason?"

"Nope. Just warning you." He looks over my shoulder and winces. "Incoming. See ya later, kid." Hudson smacks my shoulder, then waves at someone. "Hey, Scarlet."

Fuck.

I turn and smile. "Hey, Mom."

Five minutes later, I'm sitting across from my Dad's desk, while Mom sits behind it and Dad stands next to her. Apparently, this day could actually get worse, and now I'm sitting in the crosshairs of hell.

"Would you care to explain exactly what you were thinking?" Mom asks.

Scarlet Kingston St. James is the master of her universe.

She's a woman who's dominated a man's world for three decades as the president of the Philadelphia Kings football franchise and vice president of King Corp., my family's multi-billion-dollar empire. She's a badass and a hard-ass to everyone in the world who's not her family. To us, she's

Mom, and to my dad, she's everything. She hates when the world doesn't bend to her iron will . . . and hates it even more when it's her kids refusing to do so.

"Not really." Okay, maybe my answer is a little too indifferent, but there's no way this goes well for me, and I can't decide if Dad's humoring her or if he agrees with her. "I'm twenty-six, Mom."

"And . . . you're still my child. And if you need to remind me you're a grown man, try considering what that says about you, not me."

"Fuck me," Dad grumbles. "Duchess, he's a grown man."

"Are you kidding me?" she snaps and pushes to her feet. "He moved in with her, Cade. There was a bomb in her dressing room less than a month ago. She has a security team surrounding her twenty-four seven. A team stacked full of people licensed to carry guns. What exactly is our son going to do to protect Lilah Ryan that her security team can't?"

Dad opens his mouth, but Mom's not done with her rant. "And aren't you supposed to be yelling at him about his fight? Shouldn't you be lecturing him about focus and consequences?"

"Mom—"

"No." She spins back to me. "My only concern is you and your safety. I don't want to hear it. I don't care what you think you're doing. You're not. She doesn't need you, and you're putting yourself in danger, playing house. Think, Killian. What are you going to do? Jump in front of a bomb for this girl you haven't seen in ten years?"

"Scarlet." Dad's voice is quiet. It's the voice we heard growing up when we knew we were in trouble. "Stop. You're allowed to be worried about him, but Kill's not a kid anymore, he's a man. One who I'm pretty sure understands what he's doing." Dad flashes me a look that says *don't open your fucking mouth, kid, or I'll skin you alive myself*. So I do as I was silently told and watch, because honest to God, nobody ever wants to fight with my mom. You never win. *Never*. And given the chance, she's not gonna like what I'm gonna say.

"Cade . . ." Mom softens, and Dad pulls her into his side. "I hate when you're calmer than me."

"Somebody has to be." He kisses her temple, then looks at me. "No distractions, Killer. Don't let me catch this interfering or I will rain hell down on you like you've never seen. And let me know if she's going to be hanging around here during the day. I'll get the extra office cleared out, so she has a space to go when you're busy."

I stare at him, with *that's it?* on the tip of my tongue.

Luckily, I'm smart enough not to ask that.

"She's got a full gym in her basement. I'd already gotten close to two hours in there before I even came in today. No distractions. My title is still my top priority." I'm supposed to mean those words. I meant them a month ago. I meant them a week ago. I'm not so sure I mean them now, and I don't know what the fuck that means.

Lilah Ryan is a friend.

Barely.

She hates my guts.

Probably has a voodoo doll that looks like me in her nightstand.

Maybe it's tucked right in there next to her vibrator.

And there go my thoughts right back to those damn shorts and those fucking legs.

I'm saved from my spiraling thoughts when one of the girls who works the front desk knocks on the door. "Cade," she calls out.

"Come on in," Dad answers.

"Umm, sorry to interrupt." She looks around the room and clearly reads the tension. "But one of the guys is bothering Lilah Ryan, and Brynlee looks like she's one step away from knocking him out cold."

"Shit," Dad and I both mutter as we push through the door.

"Maybe we should set up her basement for you to do more of your training there." Dad grabs my arm and yanks me back when I see the asshole getting his ass handed to him by Brynlee. "Let's talk about it after your mother leaves."

Whatever Brynn says to the dude has him hanging his head and walking away, sulking like a puppy dog someone just kicked. My sister, however, looks disappointed she didn't get to kick his ass.

Then there's Lilah.

Lilah, who looks scared until she sees me.

Her wide eyes settle, and her head lifts just a bit. It's a mix between a brave face and relief, and that, right there, is why I agreed to all the bullshit that's no doubt coming my way. Because that girl is the same girl who used to feel safe when she was with me just because it was me. That girl is still in there, and that means I've still got a chance to find that girl again. If she'll let me in.

Lilah
♪♫

Chapter 11

You'll always be my favorite once upon a time,
even if you can never be my happily ever after ...
Now that's a good lyric.

—Lilah's Secret Thoughts

KILLIAN

Gonna be a few more hours at the gym. You
still at home?

LILAH

Yeah. Tasha is here going over a few things.

KILLIAN

The hot assistant?

LILAH

No banging my assistant, asshole.

*P*lease, sweet baby Jesus, do not let him actually want to bang my assistant.

I tease the rest of the guys about it. But not him. Him, I might actually castrate if he were to go there. Yup. Slowly. Then I'd fire her.

KILLIAN

Worry about Maverick or Jamie, not me, princess. I'm in training, remember.

LILAH

And?

KILLIAN

No distractions. Girls are distractions.

LILAH

Women stop liking being referred to as girls by the time they're twenty, St. James.

KILLIAN

Do you live to drive me insane?

LILAH

Maybe . . .

KILLIAN

You do a really good job of it.

Don't leave without Xander or one of the guys.

LILAH

I don't need a babysitter.

KILLIAN

Then why have I been living at your house for two weeks?

LILAH

I thought it was the gym in my basement.

KILLIAN

Well, it's sure as shit not for your stunning personality.

Stay home, please.

Infuriating. Completely. Totally. Utterly infuriating.

He knows if he asks nicely, it's harder for me to say no.

He's also been insanely overprotective the past few days since someone tried to scale the fence and get onto the property in the middle of the night. Xander's team handled it and told me about it the next day, and Killian basically lost his mind. As if waking us up at two a.m. after it was handled was the better move. What would that have done except scare me to death and make sure I was awake the rest of the night?

I silence my phone and toss it aside, then give my full attention back to my assistant, Tasha.

"Okay, your final fitting for your birthday dress is tomorrow. The party is Saturday, which is your birthday." Tasha checks off her list, like it's her favorite thing in the world to do. I'm pretty sure her lists have lists. Wish I was half as organized as she is.

"Really?" I tease. "The party is Saturday?"

"Yes," she answers in all seriousness, like Saturday isn't Valentine's Day. Also known as Noah's and my birthday. "Oh, right. That one you knew."

"Yup," I laugh. "One of the few things I manage to remember." The teapot whistles, and I move around my kitchen, grabbing my honey and lemon. "Would you like a cup?"

"No. I'm good, thanks." Her fingers fly across the keyboard of her MacBook before she stops and looks up again. "Did you need me to pick up anything for Noah?"

"Nope. I've got him covered." I squeeze my lemon in my tea and drizzle way too much honey before I stir and sip. Ahh . . . soup is comfort food for some people. For me, it's tea with honey and lemon.

"Perfect." The intercom system in the house beeps, followed by Xander's voice. "Mr. Beneventi is here to see you, Lilah."

"Which Mr. Beneventi, Xander? There's a ton of them." I swear, he needs to get laid so he'll lighten up. Hmm . . . I look over at Tasha . . . Maybe there is one person who could be allowed to bang my assistant.

"Lilah, let me through the gate. It's cold out here," I hear Maverick's voice carry through the speaker.

"Hi, Aunt Tink," a little voice chimes in, and I'm suddenly giddy and ready to toss aside all my plans for the day. I mean, if I had any, I'd throw those bitches through the window for that sweet voice.

"Well, if it isn't my favorite rose. You should have said it was you, Rosie. Why don't you leave your daddy outside and you come in and give me a squeeze."

Beautiful tinkling laughter comes through the speaker as I hear the beep of the gate rising. "We can't leave Daddy outside."

The line goes dead, and I know Maverick's heading up to the house.

"I think that's it for the day, Tasha. Thanks for your help. I'll see you Saturday." I take a sip of my tea and wait for her to pack up. Tasha has been with me for a few years, and she's great, but I don't mix my family and work, and Mav and Briar Rose are firmly planted in the family category, even if not by blood.

I think I see a flash of annoyance cross her face, but I can't be sure because it's gone as fast as it appeared. "Great. Thank you, Lilah. Let me know if you need anything else."

"Tink . . ." Maverick's booming voice is followed by a knock on the door before it opens. "Son of a nutcracker, Tink." Maverick lets himself in my house as Tasha and I move into the foyer. Mav sees Tasha and scoops Rosie up on his hip, then glares at who he considers a stranger in his presence. One of the only people I've ever met more private than me is Maverick, and it's because of that little girl.

"A nutcracker?" Tasha asks, and I think Mav actually growls.

"Be nice, Daddy," Rosie tells him as she rests her head on his shoulder. "Mimi says you have to work on that."

I smother my laughter. I swear Mav's mom has been saying he should work on that his whole life. He only finds alternative ways to curse because he doesn't want to use adult words in front of Rosie. I try to watch myself, but I slip at least once every time I see her. If I have kids one day, their first word is definitely going to be *fuck*, and it's absolutely going to be my fault.

"I'm just going to take that as my cue to leave," Tasha announces awkwardly before she waves and lets herself out.

Once the door is closed behind her, Mav throws the lock and puts Rosie down. "Was she the last one to come in, Tink?"

I nod, and his eyes darken. "If she leaves that door unlocked again, fire her. I don't care how much security you have." He looks down at Rosie and palms her head like a basketball, then runs his hand over her soft hair. No one would know this big, tough football player, who just won the Super Bowl two weeks ago, could be such a softie for his kid, mainly because the world doesn't even know Briar Rose exists, and Maverick has no intention of changing that any time soon.

I ignore Maverick and his impending lecture and squat

down next to one of my most favorite little girls and bop her on the nose. "Hey, Rosie, do you know what I have?"

She shakes her head excitedly.

"I have ice cream."

Her cherubic face falls with disappointment. "I can't have ice cream, Aunt Tink."

I look at her father and wink before looking back at Rosie. "Oh, ye of little faith . . ."

"Ye of what who?" she asks, confused.

I pop up on my feet and take her hand in mine. "It just means trust me. Aunt Tink has you covered."

"But I don't want to be covered. The splotches itch, and they always come if I have ice cream."

This poor kid. She's four years old and already knows not to touch dairy, wheat, or nuts. Tree nuts and peanuts. But the peanuts are the worst. The others will give her a horrible rash. But the peanuts—that one is deadly.

I guarantee Maverick has two epi pens in the backpack he's got hanging from one shoulder. I know there's at least another one in his car. His parents have two at their house, and everyone in Rosie's sphere knows the rules. We have to. No slipups. Never.

Noah and I were on tour the only time she's ever needed her epi pens, and she needed them both. Two Halloweens ago, she was having her weekly visitation with her mother and helped herself to a peanut butter cup from her mom's purse. Thank God the social worker was there, monitoring the visit, and acted fast or it could have been a very different thing. As it was, they kept Rosie in the hospital overnight. I can't imagine what that had to be like for her or him.

"Tink . . ." Maverick warns as we walk into the kitchen.

"You can check the ingredients yourself, big Daddy. But I promise you, I checked. It hasn't been opened, and you know me. There is not a peanut substance to be found in this house." I grab the carton out of the fridge and pass it to Maverick, then sit Rosie on my counter and grab two spoons. "Look good?"

"Does it, Daddy?"

Mav smiles, and Rosie cheers.

"I have strawberries we can add too," I tell her and kiss her cheek.

My front door opens again, and I glance over at the security cameras displayed on the corner counter of the kitchen. Noah. "Tink . . ." he calls out.

Rosie's eyes get big and excited. "She's back here, Uncle Noah."

"Is that my favorite girl?"

She nods, and I melt.

"Well, look what the cat dragged in," he says to Mav once he walks into the kitchen, Baby's case in his hand.

"Nope. No cats, Uncle Noah. I'm allergic to them too."

He goes to the kitchen sink and washes his hands, then picks her up and drops a kiss on her head. "Hey, Rosie Posie. Want to help Tink and me write a song?"

"Ohh . . ." She looks at Mav. "Can I, Daddy?"

"You'll probably do a better job than he will, sweetheart." Mav leans in, like he's about to tell her the greatest secret in the world. "He's not that good. I heard Aunt Lilah does all the hard work."

I dig my spoon into the ice cream and hide my smile. "This is why you're my favorite."

"I'm the hottest one too," Mav waggles his dark brows, and Rosie cracks up.

"Are you sick, Daddy? It's not hot in here. Do you have a fever?"

The three of us try to hold in our laughter, but we lose the fight, and instead of being upset, Rosie joins in with us. I don't think she has a clue what she's laughing at, but she's laughing with her whole heart the way only little kids can.

Later, when Jamie shows up, I smell a rat. A big, fat, stupid rat, who doesn't want me home alone for a few hours. One who's getting harder to keep locked in the safe little box I've had him shoved in for a decade.

But as I sit on the floor with Rosie in my lap, and Jamie and Mav in front of the TV playing *Madden*, I'm happy. Truly happy.

With Noah on my couch, strumming a new chord, while Rosie and I try to put words to the music, I can't seem to remember why I'm supposed to be mad.

Killian

*J*t's after eight by the time I get back to Lilah's that night. Today was fucking grueling. The kind of day you think might never end. But when I walk into her house and hear her laughing, I might just breathe a little easier. She doesn't do that as much as she used to.

Laughter . . . I never knew it was something you could take for granted.

I drop my bag by the steps and follow the sound to the edge of the family room, and what I see stops me cold. Lilah and the guys are all stretched out on her couch, while the end credits of *The Hangover* roll over the fucked up evidence of Wolfpack's night in Las Vegas. Rosie is tucked against Lilah, sleeping with her head against her chest and her fingers wrapped around her hair. These two are the perfect picture of pure love and innocence, and fuck me, it hits me hard. Harder than it should.

I'm not sure how long I stand there watching them, but the next thing I know, the commercials are rolling, and everyone is walking toward me. Rosie's in Maverick's arms now, and Lilah is ignoring me as she chats with Jamie. She looks at me and dismisses me just as quickly as everyone else says their goodbyes.

Lilah walks the guys to the front of the house, while Noah puts his bass away in a case and locks it. He grabs the handle but moves in front of me, then waits.

"What's up, man?" I ask, too fucking tired to deal with people.

Even my people.

"Good call, letting us know she was going to be alone all day."

"No problem. She just didn't feel like going to Crucible today, and I had to go. I can do a lot in the gym downstairs, but not everything. She's probably pissed at me." Not that I'm shocked.

"She's always pissed at you." Noah shrugs, but there's something about the rigid way he's holding himself. The line of his shoulders. Like he's coiled tight. "You gonna tell me what's going on with you and my sister?"

That's it.

There's the strike.

Fast and brutal, like a snake bite.

"What are you talking about? Spit it out, man. I'm tired. And let's not forget you asked me to do this." I look toward the foyer but can't see Lilah.

"I didn't ask you to look at her like you were looking," he groans.

"Jesus, Noah. How the fuck do you think I was looking at

her?" I don't know what the hell he's going on about, and I'm so far over it and this day, I don't even give a shit.

"You were looking like she was your world . . ." When I don't answer him, he steps back with a curse. "Be careful, Killer. I'm not standing here warning you off. That's not how we are. But I'm telling you if you hurt her, I don't give a shit how tough you are. I'll make you fucking regret you ever met her."

"You think I don't know how much easier this would all be if—Shit. *Shit*. It would be easier." Damn, it would be easier.

"What would?" Lilah asks as she enters the kitchen behind us.

Noah drops a kiss on his sister's head. "Nothing, Tink. Lock up behind me. And send me the rest of the lyrics I know you wrote while Rosie was sleeping."

"They sucked, Noah," she sighs, and the tightness in her shoulders and neck snap into place.

"You've got to get past this block at some point. Might as well try now. Maybe it'll help." He pulls his keys from his pocket and auto-starts his car. "'Night, guys."

Lilah waits for the front door to click shut, then turns to the security system on the counter and arms it. "I'm going to make more tea. Do you want some?"

"No, thanks." In the next room, I hear *The Hangover Part Two* starting. "Want to watch a movie with me?"

I shouldn't ask.

We've stayed as far apart as two people living together can get away with since our first morning together. I've spent those weeks trying to convince myself it's what we needed. Neither of us splitting focus on the important things in our own lives while we coexisted and stuck to our agreement. But I'm already tired of lying to myself. This woman . . . *Fuck* . . . I take her hand in mine and drag her gently to the couch. "Come on, princess."

I drop down into the oversized cushions and pull her down with me.

"I hate that nickname," she whispers as something stirs in her cobalt eyes. Darker than the stars shining in through the giant wall of windows surrounding us.

"No, you don't," I whisper back and grab her favorite blanket from the back of the couch and wrap it around her.

Twenty minutes into the movie, she's sound asleep and lightly snoring.

Thirty minutes in, and her head is on my chest the way Rosie's was on hers earlier.

By the halfway mark, I lift her in my arms and carry her to bed.

I try to convince myself it's because I don't want to wake her.

Lilah has always looked like an angel when she slept.

But as I walk up the stairs with her in my arms and her head resting on my shoulder, I know it's more than that. So fucking much more. The way she feels against me. Peace and warmth and home and hope all wrapped up in one beautiful woman.

I walk into her room and am assaulted by everything Lilah. Her scent surrounds me, and the pictures on her dresser assault me. The five of us in high school. Dillan and her at the beach. Rosie and her at one of Lilah's concerts. Bright pink noise-canceling headphones on Rosie's small head, beaded bracelets up and down her little arms, and the biggest smile I've ever seen on her face.

I force myself to move and pull down her white blanket, then lay her in her bed.

My fingers caress the curve of her face before I lean down and kiss her forehead. "Sleep, princess. No one will ever hurt you again. Not even me." The words are a whispered promise. They might as well be a sacred oath for as much as I mean every single one of them.

When I stand, she rolls to her side and tucks her hands under her face unconsciously and murmurs, "Do you swear, Killian?"

"With my life, Lilah." I drag my finger down her face again, then pull the blanket up and tuck her in. "With my life . . ."

The Philly Press

VALENTINES DAY DELIGHT

Happy Valentine's Day, Kroydon Hills. Love is in the air, and celebrities have invaded our town. Rumors are swirling that Lilah Ryan is hosting the party of the year tonight at West End. And in typical megastar fashion, our favorite hot spot is closed to the public. Guess they're trying to keep out prying eyes. But fear not, you know I have my ways and will bring all the glamorous play-by-plays. If we're lucky, maybe one of our hockey hotties will take home a certain pop star princess. If we're really lucky, maybe it'll be two.

#KroydonKronicles #PopPrincess #ValentinesDayDelight

Killian

Chapter 12

The twins have always done something big for their birthday. Noah used to bitch because it's Valentine's Day. His mom would get them each their own heart-shaped cake from Sweet Temptations, and Noah would act like he hated it, while Lilah looked at that cake every year like it was the most perfect thing in the world. He claims he never said a word to his mom because he didn't want to change the tradition for Lilah, but I'm pretty sure he loved those cakes too. Maybe not as much as his sister. But still . . .

Guess we've all been wrapped around her little finger most of her life.

Case in point, I slide my wallet in my jeans and grab the small pink box wrapped in the red heart ribbon from the dresser. This present might just be one of the dumbest ideas I've ever had, but it's time.

She's the only person I've ever played nice for, and I'm about done playing.

I step out of my room, surprised to see Lilah's door open. She's spent the past two days avoiding me. Guess things got a little too real the other night, so she went back into hiding like the groundhog who saw his shadow. She'd knee me in the balls if she heard me compare her to a fucking groundhog, and that puts an extra swagger in my step.

She's either gonna love this and maybe cry or she's gonna hate it and throw it at me . . . *again*.

I knock on the open door and look around her empty room.

This door is never open.

Never.

"Birthday girl . . . you in here?" I don't step inside her space. Not uninvited.

Yeah . . . nice is getting old.

"I'm coming," she calls out in a breathy voice, and I'd like her to be saying those words, just like that, for a very different reason. My cock jumps, and I adjust myself before she walks out of her bathroom, barefoot, in the sexiest goddamned dress I've ever seen. It's sheer and covered in tiny shimmery threads covering a nude slip that hugs every fucking curve. The sheer fabric barely covers her ass, and I'm thinking I'm going to be kicking more than one guy's ass for looking at her tonight. At least it covers her up above her collarbone. If I'm going to be picturing her naked all fucking night, she's doing me a solid and not teasing me with what I'm going to bet are the most perfect tits I've ever seen.

"Hey, St. James." She snaps her fingers, then points from me to her eyes. "My eyes are up here."

"Fucking princess," I growl.

"I hate that nickname," she murmurs but smiles the tiniest bit.

"No, you don't," I tell her and step into her space, holding the pink gift box out for her. "Happy birthday, Lilah."

She wrinkles her brow as she stares at the box in my hand. "What's that?"

"A birthday gift, Lilah. Want to take it from me?" Sarcasm flows right under my words, and her bright blue eyes stare, focused on my hand.

"I'm not sure," she finally answers, and fuck, that hurts.

I take her hand in mine and gently turn it over, palm up, then place the small box on her open palm. "It's not going to bite, princess."

She opens her mouth to argue but stops and drags her teeth over her pouty bottom lip instead. "I guess it's too small to be a snake."

"Yeah. Little bit," I laugh. "You don't have to open it now."

That seems to settle her as she studies it some more.

One perfectly painted white nail traces the ribbon. "Did you wrap this?"

"Brynn helped with the bow," I admit. I don't tell her my sister cornered me the other day and asked what I was getting Lilah for her birthday.

"It's pretty." She finally looks up, and damn . . . this woman. When she lets those defenses down, she takes incredible to a whole new level. "Thank you."

"You going to open it?" I push, and her perfectly white teeth press into that lip again as she shakes her head.

Fuck me.

"Okay," I lower my voice and lay off the teasing for once. "When you're ready."

Lilah places it gently on her vanity and turns to slip her feet into red-soled, sparkly shoes, giving me my first taste of the back of that damn dress. And ho-ly shit. There is no back. A single sparkly strand ties between her shoulders with the ends of the ribbon trailing down her bare spine. Her completely bare spine. All the way down to the dimples right above her heart-shaped ass where the fabric gathers and pools. Visions of snapping the string with my fucking teeth play out behind my eyes, followed by every filthy thing I want to do to her after.

Lilah turns back to me in a flourish, and my heart gets stuck in my throat. "You are so pretty, it hurts, princess."

Her beautiful smile disappears as quickly as it appeared, and I feel like the biggest dick in the world.

"Yeah . . . well, hopefully someone who doesn't get off on the pain will think so too. I'm going to have Xander drive me. Are you coming?"

I slide my hand to the small of her back, letting her soft, warm skin calm the rage I feel over hearing those words. "Those are fighting words, Lilah."

She bristles under my touch. "It's what we do best, isn't it, Killer?"

I lean down and brush my lips over her ear, and my chest fucking roars when goose bumps dance down her skin. "According to you, we lie best, and we need to put on a hell of a show tonight, don't we? I mean, if we want anyone outside our circle to think we're dating, we're going to have to act like we're in love."

Her long lashes flutter rapidly as she blinks up at me, trying to gain control over her composure. Good luck with that. Mine's been shot for weeks now.

"Let them think we're hate-fucking. The sex is probably better that way anyway." She steps out of my grasp and looks over her shoulder. "I mean . . . it's not like the thought never crossed my mind."

What the fuck?

"You what?" I choke.

Her eyes trail over me, lingering over the obvious bulge in my jeans. "We both know I wanted you to fuck me back in the day." She closes the distance between us and trails a finger down my chest. "I thought I loved you then." Her hand stops on my belt, and I swear to God, I'm ready to bend her over right here, right fucking now. "But even if I know I hate you now, you're still hot, St. James. I bet you'd look real nice with me on my knees in front of you."

She spins away abruptly and walks out of the room.

111

"Car is leaving in five minutes, Killer. If you're going to jerk off to that image, you better make it quick."

Lilah

"*L*ilah." Xander clears his throat as he pulls to a stop at the red light down the street from West End. His eyes search me out through the rearview mirror. "Front or back door?"

With Killian next to me back here, I'm feeling a little more brave than I have recently. What the hell? Guess it's now or never. "You ready to make our debut, champ?"

"Consider me ready and willing to meet all your needs, princess."

Oh, he's good.

That little show in my bedroom was more fun than I thought it would be, and I'd be totally lying to myself if I didn't admit that I've thought about it a whole lot since he came back into my life. Not as much as I did in high school, but enough that hate-screwing him is what I see when I close my eyes at night and reach for my vibrator.

Why do the biggest assholes have to be the hottest men?

"Sounds like it's gonna be the front door, Xander."

Xander shakes his head and glares. "Do you have your panic button?"

I tug it from my purse and hold it up, then swap it out for a compact and touch up my lip gloss as the light switches to green, and Xander pulls us up to the line of people waiting for their chance to get inside Maddox's bar.

They're going to be waiting all night.

The bar is closed to the public tonight.

Noah and I rented it out so we could celebrate with our friends and family in private.

I'm pretty sure we're going to be testing the city fire code with the maximum capacity anyway. Last I checked, Noah had invited half the damn town and half our damn tour. Dancers, singers, the band, the stagehands. He kind of missed the small party memo, but it's his birthday too, so I went with it.

The Rover rolls to a stop, and Xander gets out of the car as Killian turns to me and frames my face. "Listen to me, princess . . . You listening?"

Damn, he's so close.

I nod, and he tilts my head back to look up at him. "You want everyone in there to think we're together, right? Part of the whole bodyguard, keep you safe thing?"

Why does his voice sound like that?

Like he's swallowed glass?

I lick my lips. "If it still works for you, it's what my label's expecting. Iris should be here tonight. Zoe and Scottie too."

"Is it what you want though?" His calloused thumb runs along my jaw, and I suddenly wonder if my thong was a serious misjudgment of choice on my part as I cross my legs and lean into him.

"Yes, St. James. It's what I want. It's what I need to get what I want, so it looks like you're stuck with me." What in the world was I thinking agreeing to this?

He leans his forehead against mine and inhales.

My lord, he smells good.

"What are you doing?" I breathe out as he breathes in, barely above a whisper.

"I'm going to have to touch you tonight, Lilah." One hand slides down my back and grips my hips while the other digs

113

into my hair. "Your man wouldn't be able to keep his hands off you."

"Really?" Holy shit, that sounded needy, even to my own ears.

He pulls me closer and lowers his face until his hot breath warms me, and his lips, lips women would pay a doctor to get but come completely naturally to Killian, nearly graze mine. "Yeah, princess."

"I hate that nickname," I whisper.

"No." His lips graze mine. "You don't."

Oh my God. Killian drops his lips to my neck, and my entire world stands still.

The noise stops, and everyone else ceases to exist as his teeth scrape my skin, and I grip the front of his shirt for dear life.

Then all at once, I climb into his lap, and the door opens, and our bubble is broken.

Well, I guess that's one way to introduce this fake relationship to the world.

"*H*ow many of those things have you had?" Dillan eyes my pink cocktail as I sip.

"Oh . . . you mean my French Kiss?" I laugh.

"What's a French Kiss?" She lifts it from my hand and sips for herself. "Ohh. That's yummy."

"Gin, St. Germain, Aperol, a squeeze of fresh lemon juice, and top it with sparkling rosé. It's delicious, right? Maddox taught me how to make it earlier." I take it back and finish it off. "And this is only my second. I don't want to get drunk and be forced to look at the pictures splashed everywhere."

The song changes, and a sultry Kings Of Leon song thrums through the speakers.

One of my backup dancers, Jeremy, moves between me and Dillan. He's more than one of my dancers. He's my friend, and I don't use that term loosely. "Come on, girl."

He takes my drink out of my hand and sits it on the bar, then takes my hand and pulls me with him. I go willingly.

Jeremy and I have been dancing on stage together for years. This man has had his hands all over my body . . . in a strictly working kind of way. I don't have the equipment he wants, which is a shame for me because he moves like he knows exactly what you need. His husband, however, appreciates it very, very much. I've heard the stories. But that's life on the road.

I'm pulled against him as the beat pulses, and his knee slides between my legs. "You want to tell me why that Adonis leaning against the bar looks like he wants to eviscerate me, Lilah? Did you go and get yourself a man? One who looks like a Hemsworth?"

"Sort of . . ." I'm not sure how to answer that, so I go vague. It feels safe.

I drape my arm over his shoulder, and Jeremy moves his hand down my back.

"Oh shit. Is he going to kick my ass, Lilah? Cause honey, this body wasn't made for fighting." Jeremy loves to stir shit up, though, so instead of moving his hand, he tightens his hold.

Why does this give me an idea?

I lean into Jeremy. "Does he look jealous?"

"No, baby girl. He looks murderous. Jealous men are insecure. This one looks like he's ready to kill me to prove a point to everyone in this room. I don't think insecure is in his vocabulary."

He spins me around and slides his hands from my hips

down my thighs as my dress lifts a little too high, and oh yeah . . . Killian's eyes lock in on mine like a heat-seeking missile, and it's fucking hot. His fists are clenched, knuckles white, and I doubt he has any idea what the hell Rome is telling him right now.

Jeremy slides my hair behind my shoulder and whispers in my ear, "How far are you planning on taking this?"

Before I get a chance to answer, his hand slides under the hem of my dress, and Killian pushes off the bar.

"Oh, fuck no, baby girl. I'm out of here. Go make up with your man." He lowers his voice as Killian crosses the room. "Suck his dick. We men like that. Don't say I didn't give you something for your birthday." A quick kiss to the cheek, and he's gone.

Once he's in front of me, I grab Killian's hands. "Dance with me, St. James."

Not needing to be told twice, one of his big arms wraps around my back and holds me close. So similar yet completely different from Jeremy. "Who was that?"

"Why, champ? You jealous?" Please let him say yes.

Oh shit. I'll need to psychoanalyze that thought tomorrow.

"Should I be?" Ugh. Of course that's his answer. It tells me nothing.

"Well." I wrap both arms around his neck and inhale that fresh ocean scent. Soap and salt and sea and all Killian for as long as I can remember. "Jealous implies ownership. You want something someone else has. First, no one has me to own, and second, you don't want me. You've demonstrated that before. So, I'd say no, you've got nothing to be jealous of."

"The fuck, Lilah?" He doesn't sound mad. No . . . he sounds hurt. "Can't you let that go? Just for tonight? It was a fucking decade ago. We were kids, and there is nothing about that weekend that I wouldn't change if I could . . . Trust me."

I lean my head on his chest and hide my eyes. "What would you say if I told you I could try. Just for tonight. Try to forget. To . . ."

He lifts my chin with his finger. "To not hate me for one night for something that happened before we were old enough to understand the consequences?"

"Yes." There are so many things I want to say, but that's the only thing I manage.

His big hand wraps around my neck as he leans down and I press up.

The kiss is strong and soft and sexy and sweet. It's mind-blowing and heart-stopping.

Before I know it, my feet are no longer touching the ground, and I'm carried off the floor. "Killian . . ." I gasp and pull my mouth back. "What are you doing?"

"Taking you home. I've wanted that kiss for years, and I'm not wasting my one night here."

"Uh-uh, champ. It's my birthday party. I can't leave yet." I don't care that everyone is staring. I don't care that I love this and hate it equally in measure. I only care that he finally, *finally*, kissed me.

"Fine." He sits me on top of the bar and moves between my legs. "But you do not move from my side all night."

"St. James . . ." I dig my fingers in his hair and ignore the catcalls coming from our friends. "I agreed to not hate you for one night. I never agreed to give up my control."

"You don't have to give up anything, princess. It's your choice. You can dance with every man here. Just be prepared for me to beat the fucking shit out of any man who looks at you. And if he fucking touches you, he's going to be pissing blood into a bag for a week. Your choice."

"Hey, Lilah?" Only Maddox Beneventi would have the

BELLA MATTHEWS

balls to tap my shoulder from behind the bar right now in the middle of this. Killian growls, actually growls, and it's fucking hot. "You ready for another French Kiss?"

"You've got to be shitting me," Killian barks, and Madman laughs.

"Chill out, cousin."

I spin around on the shiny bar and hop down behind it, putting it between Killian and me. "Yeah, chill out, champ. It's a drink Maddox taught me how to make. And yes, I'd love another."

"Don't get drunk, Lilah," Killian warns me.

Oh. Hell. No.

"Hey Maddox?" I call out while I stare right at Killian. "Want to do a shot with me?"

"You're the birthday girl, Tink. How about I make a pink one up just for you."

"Lilah—"

Oh, this is going to be fun.

Killian

Chapter 13

*S*he did two shots and has been sipping the same frothy pink drink for the past two hours. Lilah's tiny, but I don't think she's drunk. What she is, is determined to drive me crazy. Instead of staying by my side, I've watched her flit around the bar like the damn fairy she's nicknamed after. Lucky for the men here tonight, she hasn't allowed any of them to get close unless they're a relative of hers or mine. That I can handle . . . *I think.*

My jaw clenches when Rome throws his arm over her shoulder, so his hand is dangling dangerously close to her breast, and looks right at me.

"Your brother has a death wish," I grumble to Maddox, knowing I'm going to make the fucker pay when we spar on Monday.

"You just now figuring that out, Killer?"

Rome leans in and whispers something to Lilah that has her turning to look at me with a mischievous smile before she blows me a kiss.

Fucking brat.

"You sure you know what you're doing, cousin?" Maddox offers me a beer, but I shake my head. "Because you look like you're about to throw that girl over your shoulder . . . Or maybe your knee."

"*Not a bad idea,*" I mumble and watch her throw her head back with laughter.

I've chased this girl once tonight. We've kissed twice. And I've been hard all fucking night long. I don't have a fucking clue what I'm doing or why I've waited a lifetime to do it. Probably should have done it when we were kids. Or at least an acceptable version of it for two high schoolers. "And the answer is no. I don't have a clue what I'm doing. Just that I want to do it more than is probably healthy."

"Fuck health. We could all be dead tomorrow from the next ice age the way the snow has been falling this winter. Just don't fuck shit up. Not with Lilah and not with Noah and the guys. Trust me."

"Yeah. I get it." When Maddox's best friend knocked up his little sister, it definitely complicated shit between our friends. "But this is just a one-night kinda truce."

The minute the words leave my mouth, I know I'm full of shit.

And as Rome slides his arm from around Lilah's shoulders down to her waist, I feel like a bull that just had a crimson red flag swung in front of it.

"Lilah doesn't seem like a one-night-truce kinda girl," Maddox warns me, like I need to be told what kind of girl Lilah is. She's the same girl who stops in the middle of the street to make sure a turtle gets safely across the road. She's the girl who volunteers at the soup kitchen with a hat pulled over her eyes and absolutely no media anywhere to be seen because she wants to, not because it looks good. She's the girl who helped me study for my driver's test and used to sit, writing songs, while I was working out at the gym, just so she didn't have to be alone.

I don't care how many years it's been. I know Lilah Ryan.

"No shit, cousin. But if I can get her to forget she hates me for one night, it's a start. And I think it's about time I take the birthday girl home before your momma gets pissed that I broke her son."

"It's his life," he laughs like an asshole. "He knows what he's doing."

"See ya, man." I push away from the bar and ignore Jamie and Noah's glares as I move between Lilah and Rome.

Guess not everyone was good with our little show earlier.

Might not want to ask me if I care though.

At least not right now.

"Excuse me," Rome bitches, like I'm stealing his favorite toy.

Sorry, buddy. She was never yours.

Even if I can't bring myself to admit it's because she was always mine.

"Fuck off, Beneventi." I replace his arm with mine, and Lilah smiles like I just did exactly what she wanted as she leans into my side. "You ready to get out of here, princess?"

Her beautiful blue eyes shine. "What took you so damn long, St. James?"

That's a great question.

"Jesus Christ. Get a room and then don't tell us about it," Jamie bitches.

I think Noah dry heaves. "Yeah. Get this shit out of the way, then go back to hating each other so everything can be right in the world, okay?"

Lilah gives them both the finger, then pulls her phone from her purse. "Just let me text Xander to bring the car around back." Her fingers fly across the screen before she looks up and smiles her prettiest smile. Not because it's perfect. Because it's real. "Done. We're outta here, bitches. See you at dinner Sunday night."

She laces her fingers with mine, and that smile eases into something different.

Something bolder.

It holds a promise and begs for relief.

I press my lips to the top of her head as we walk through the crowd and into the back hall. "I thought I told you to stick by my side."

Lilah laughs, having absolutely no clue what she's doing to me . . . or maybe she does. "Yes, you did, champ. You gonna punish me?"

"Fuck, Lilah. You can't say that shit to me." I crowd her up against the wall. "Christ, woman. Do you have any idea what you're doing to me?"

I stretch her wrists over her head and hold them as I drag my lips up the long column of her neck, my body pressing against hers. The hard length of my cock against her stomach. The heat rolling off us in waves. "Every single time you smiled that smart mouth my way, I thought about fucking you, princess. Is that what you want to hear? Is that what you're trying to do to me?"

Lilah's breath stutters, and she licks her lips for a hot second before she leans into the wall and uses it to balance so she can wrap her legs around my waist.

Holy fucking hell.

I drop her hands and dig my fingers into her bare ass under this joke of a dress. She might as well be naked behind the sparkles because it's all I've been picturing since the first second I saw her in it.

Her arms wrap around my neck, and her teeth graze my ear. "That's exactly what I was hoping for . . ."

The door to Maddox's office opens, one I hadn't even realized we were standing nearly on top of, and my room-mate Bellamy walks out, followed by a smiling Maverick. "Uh . . . you didn't see anything."

Lilah buries her face in my neck, giggling, until she gasps when my finger slips under her thong. Her wet thong.

"Not a fucking thing, buddy." I wait for him to walk by, then take Lilah's lips again. "You're the only thing I saw."

Lilah

*T*he drive home is a master class in exquisite torture.

Killian and I sit side by side in the back seat of the Rover, touching—but not.

Wanting, but holding back.

My bare, crossed legs pressed against his jean-clad thigh.

His big arm resting on the back of the seat, fingers teasing the nape of my neck.

We're not looking at each other for fear one of us may jump.

And my bigger fear is that *one* may be *me*.

My biggest fear, however, is that this is one gigantic mistake.

That I'm thinking with my head and not my heart.

My head can rationalize us giving in tonight and hating him again tomorrow.

My heart isn't so sure that's possible.

Not when this is what I've always wanted. Maybe even when I hated him. Definitely before.

Once we're past my gate and Xander is parked, he looks back in the rearview mirror. "Are you in for the night, Lilah?" His hard eyes flash between Killian and me when I nod. "Understood."

Killian gets out, blocking Xander from opening the door for me and takes my hand. "I've got her, thanks."

Heat prickles my skin with the touch of his rough palm, and I drag my teeth over my lower lip to keep from making a joke about Killian marking his territory like a dog. We may have a twenty-four-hour truce, but old habits die hard, and I feel like he just peed a ring around me.

"Looks like Xander isn't your biggest fan, St. James." Okay, I had to tease a little.

"He wants to fuck you." Killian's big palm swallows the entire span of my back, making me wonder just how big the rest of him is. "I wouldn't like me either tonight if I were him. Now, ask me if I care."

"I've got a pretty good idea of the answer," I giggle as I unlock the door and disable the alarm, just before Killian spins us so my back is flat against the wall . . . again.

His pupils are blown wide with need, nearly eclipsing his green irises, but he doesn't touch me. Just crowds me. "Tell me you're good with this, Lilah."

Holy shit. His voice . . . It's barely controlled and so . . . hot.

"One night, St. James . . ." I answer, nearly not recognizing my own lust-drunk voice.

His chest moves with the deep exhale that leaves him, and my entire body tenses and tightens with anticipation. "*One night* . . . Fuck, princess. One night isn't going to be enough."

He threads his fingers through my hair and holds me still while those eyes focus on something he sees reflected in mine. The look, so damn desperate and yet so utterly alpha that I fight desperately to cling to some semblance of control.

And for the second time tonight, I regret the tiny scrap of lace I chose as lingerie.

His scent wraps around me like a drug, and my God, I need another hit.

I tilt my chin up in defiance, and Killian moves his face closer. His lips hovering above mine, daring me to fight him.

I've waited my whole life for him to kiss me, and now that I know what it feels like, I may never want to stop.

Damn him.

"I hate that nickname," I pant.

Yup. Pant. Because that's what he does to me.

"No." He drops one hand to my thigh and drags his fingers up and under my dress. "*You*." His fingers slide between my legs and over my damp panties. "Don't. *Princess*."

My thong is pushed aside, and he slowly strokes my sex.

"So stop lying to yourself and to me." He traces me and drags his fingers around my thrumming clit. "Because your body doesn't lie."

"Hmmm . . ." I hum deep in my throat and hold onto his shoulders for dear life as my knees threaten to buckle when he finally pushes one blunt finger inside me.

Oh. My. God.

My body burns for more.

For him

"Jesus, Lilah. You're so tight." He pulls out and runs my juices back up to my clit and smiles when I shake. "So hot."

Stars burst behind my eyes with a sudden overwhelming need like never before, and I drag his face down and attack his lips. Tasting. Teasing. Rolling my tongue with his, so fucking needy that all rational thought leaves me momentarily as he rips another whimper from my chest.

"So tight . . ."

I pull him back to my face. "Just imagine how good it's gonna feel when you're inside me."

"Fuck, princess . . . You're killing me. Do I still need to be worried about your virtue staying intact?"

I laugh, then moan as he stretches me with a second finger. "My virtue has been gone for years. It could have been yours, but you missed out on that, champ."

He yanks his fingers free from my body, and I cry out

from the loss before he brings them to my mouth and traces my lips. "Open."

Holy. Shit.

I do as I'm told, and Killian presses his finger against my tongue.

Ohh . . . That's hot.

"No talk of the past tonight, or everything stops." He pulls his fingers away and drops to his knees with a devilish grin.

The devil you know.

And wow, this devil is more intoxicating than any cocktail I've ever had.

No man should look that good staring up at you.

Like a fucking Greek god. The god of sex.

"Nod if you agree, Lilah."

His hands slide my dress up around my waist, then grip the thin nude strings of my thong resting on my hips. "Nod, Lilah."

I slam my head back against the wall, needing the support. Afraid I'm about to crash. This is such an epically bad idea, but I don't care. Hate him or not, it was always supposed to be this . . . us. Damn it. I'm strung so tight, if he breathes on me the right way, I might just come.

The need in his eyes.

The strength in the way he's holding his body back . . . waiting for my okay.

My permission. Damn him.

I nod, and Killian rips my panties in half.

Jesus Christ. Literally snaps the strings from my body.

He lifts one leg over his shoulder in a beautifully smooth move, and I force the idea of him doing this with another woman out of my head. I dig my hands into his hair as he drags his nose up my leg.

"Such a pretty pussy, princess. Now open those eyes and

lock 'em on me. I want you to watch what I'm going to do to you."

Of course he's good at dirty talk.

Two big, wet fingers spread me, and this man drags his flattened tongue up the length of my pussy and sucks my clit. Then he drags his teeth over it and bites. *Bites.* Bursts of light flash behind my eyes, and my body convulses as I come violently, without any control.

That's it.

That's all it takes for my world to stop spinning and tilt off its axis.

Killian licks and sucks me through one orgasm, then adds one finger, then another until I'm screaming as another orgasm rips through me and my knees give out.

"Knew you'd be pretty when you come, princess." He stands, lifting me in his arms, then takes my mouth with his in the hottest kiss of my life. Of. My. Life.

Tasting myself on his lips, I want to drop to my knees and return the favor, but Killian has other plans as he carries me up my winding staircase, like you'd carry a bride across a threshold.

"In case you ever wondered what I picture when I'm jerking off, know it's that," he growls against my lips. "I've pictured you so many times with my cock in my hand. Me fucking you. The way your tits would bounce. You on your knees with your ass in the air." He sucks my tongue, and I feel the tingle down to my toes. "The taste of you on my tongue. So pretty, princess."

"I—" I start to answer, but he cuts me off.

"No, you don't."

Killian

Chapter 14

*J*lift Lilah in my arms and take the stairs two at a time. I need this woman spread out on a bed. Not up against a wall. I need to see her. Touch her. Fucking devour her.

Without asking, I kick open her bedroom door and stop. "You still with me?"

Christ, let her still be with me.

"Put me down, St. James," she whispers wickedly. "Let me show you exactly how with you I am."

I set her on the floor, and Lilah's smile is instantaneous. "You know . . ." She spreads her palms out flat against my chest and drags them out to my shoulders and down my arms, then back up, unfastening each button with painstakingly slow precision. "That pretty picture I painted earlier . . ."

"Fuck, Lilah . . ." Her nails scrape my skin as she shoves my shirt off me. "I'll never forget that picture."

"I might have fantasized about that a time or two too . . ."

She leans in and teases my nipple with her nail, then her tongue, while she pulls my belt free from my pants. "Or maybe two hundred." She shoves my jeans and boxers down, then licks her lips. "Jesus, Killer, you're huge."

Part of me roars in triumph, part of me wants to kill any

other man she's seen naked. Either way, both parts fade away to a distant background noise when she drops to her knees with a sexy-as-sin smile on her face and my cock in her hands. She looks up at me through long dark lashes and lidded eyes, so fucking pretty.

"I've imagined doing this," she whispers quietly. "Tell me you have too."

"Fuck, Lilah. I've imagined you just like this since I figured out how to jerk myself off." I cup her face and rub my thumb over her jaw. "Open up for me, princess."

Without any hesitation, she parts her pouty pink lips and swirls her tongue around the head of my throbbing cock. She fists the base, and an arrogant smile tugs at my lips when her hand can't quite wrap entirely around me.

Lilah licks me from base to tip, then swallows me down her throat and gags.

Her eyes water, and her lashes flutter as she looks up at me—and ho-ly shit—the sight of this woman on her knees threatens every fucking ounce of control I've spent a lifetime building. I force myself to hold back and not lose control. Instead, I wrap her hair around one fist and tug gently.

"I don't want to come in your mouth, princess."

She reaches up and digs her nails into my bare ass and moans as she bats those fucking lashes. Taking me deeper into her throat. Sucking me down.

"Fuck," I growl as a thundering need builds to a roar at the base of my spine. I thrust into her mouth, giving in to the need, and Lilah cries out.

Fuck—*Fuck*—Fuck.

She licks up the length of my cock, then pops off and drags her teeth over her lips. "God, yes," she moans again before taking me down her throat and humming.

Her hot tears pool in her eyes, and I drop her hair and grab her face as my abs pull tight, with the force it's taking to maintain control. After two more strokes of her tongue, I lift her, and she wraps her legs around my waist, teasing my cock with her soaked pussy.

Lilah grinds her hips against me as she pushes her tongue into my mouth and wraps her arms around my neck. "That was even hotter than I imagined."

"Fuck, princess." My mind spins, but I force it to slow. "Condoms?"

She nips my lips as her nails score my skin. "Nightstand," she gasps as she teases me and takes me inside her . . . Just the fucking tip, and I swear to all that's holy I could come right now. "Hurry."

"No," I groan and squeeze her ass. "If I'm only getting one night with you, I'm not gonna hurry a goddamned thing."

"Always such a bossy asshole." Her words are a whimper and a protest as she sinks further down my cock. "But my God, you feel so fucking good. Fuck me, Killian."

I drop her to the bed with a bounce and open her drawer, fumbling for the condoms. I pull one out and hold it up, then toss it aside. "Baby, that's not gonna fit. I gotta go get one from my room."

When I take a step back, she sits up and pulls her dress off, leaving her naked and perfect on the bed, rocking me to my fucking core. "I'm on the pill," she pants and climbs up to her knees. "Please, please, please, just fuck me. I'm clean. I haven't had sex in so long, and I've been tested since."

"Lilah . . ." I grab the back of her neck and close my mouth over hers, swallowing her protests. "I'll be back in just a minute."

She reaches between us and squeezes my cock. "I've never been bare with anyone, Killer. Please give me this."

"Fuck, princess. I never could tell you no." I lay her back on the bed and settle between her thighs.

"Liar," she whispers and drops her knees to the bed.

I lift one foot and kiss her perfectly toned calf, then drape it over my shoulder and bury my face in her pussy.

"Shit—Killian . . ."

I drag my eyes to hers and smile against her. "Want me to stop?"

"Don't you dare. . ." She whines and lifts her hips.

"Yes, princess," I growl against her cunt and suck her clit harder each time she squirms.

"Oh God." She bows off the bed, grasping my hair. "Please . . . Please, please, please."

The sound of Lilah Ryan begging is the absolute hottest fucking thing I've ever heard.

I suck and lick and graze with my fucking teeth until she can't take it anymore, and then I stuff three fingers inside her sweet pussy and bite down and tug on her clit, and Lilah comes so hard, she sobs and falls against the bed.

"Open those eyes, princess. I'm not done with you yet."

Her beautiful cobalt eyes slowly open, sex-dazed and heavy-lidded.

Desperate.

So fucking needy.

My girl wants more.

"Killian . . ." she sighs as I kiss my way back up her body, and her legs wrap around my waist. My cock pulsing against her swollen sex. Teasing her.

She drags her fingers along the muscles of my bare back, her nails raking my skin, and drags her lips along my earlobe, then bites. "More."

I push in the tiniest bit, and she clamps down. Holding me closer. Tighter.

Bringing me closer. Faster. And I push all the way in and freeze.

"So fucking tight, Lilah. Fuck. You're squeezing the life out of me."

She whimpers and closes her eyes.

"Eyes on me, princess." I slide back out, and her eyes fly wide open and lock on mine as I push back in. "Fucking perfect, Lilah. Your cunt was made for me, baby."

"Oh God . . ." she moans as I slide my arms around her and change our angle. Setting a fast rhythm, and she matches thrust for fucking thrust.

"So fucking pretty when you come with my mouth on your cunt. Now, you're gonna show me how pretty you are when you come on my cock, aren't you, princess?" Devouring her mouth with mine, I swallow her moan . . . Her breath . . . Her fucking soul.

The word *mine* is like a war cry chanting in my mind.

Every inch of this woman has always been mine.

She knows it too, even if she can't admit it yet.

She digs her heels into my ass as our bodies slide together. Not a whisper of space between us. We're both desperate for more as our hands move everywhere. Grabbing and scraping and tugging and grinding.

Both of us barely breathing.

Her orgasm still dripping between us.

Neither ready for this to be over. *Not yet.*

Not ever.

Trailing my mouth down her body, I lick the salty sweat from her skin and suck a pretty pink nipple into my mouth.

She drags her nails down my spine to my ass and digs in and whimpers as I slam into her.

"You ready to give me what I want, Lilah?"

Her hooded eyes threaten to close.

"Keep 'em open, princess. Watch me fuck you. See how hot you are when you take my cock and watch how much I want you."

Her trembling legs tighten around me. "Fuck, Killian . . ."

I take her mouth in a demanding kiss, my tongue

stroking hers, urgent and frenzied and desperate to give us what we need, then roll us so Lilah straddles my waist. Her back arched and her hands pressed against my chest. Soft, golden-blonde hair falling around her shoulders in wild curls, covering her flawless goddamned tits.

A shy shimmer catches in her eyes as she adjusts herself, my cock still hard inside her. She lifts up on her knees, then inches down slowly.

So fucking slowly.

Wide eyes lock on mine as my hands slide to her hips, my fingertips biting into her soft skin. The vision of her like this burning itself forever into my brain. "You take my cock like such a good girl, princess."

The most perfect sound I've ever heard slips past her pouty lips as she rocks her hips in time with mine. "Oh God, Killian . . ."

Her hips move faster, and her nails claw my chest. Her breasts bounce with each movement, and I hold on like the luckiest motherfucker in the world. Because this—this woman—this night—nothing will ever be better than this.

I lift my hips and hit a different angle, and Lilah screams and tightens around me.

"Fuck, princess. You gonna come for me again? You gonna milk my cock, Lilah?"

She tenses around me and gasps such a pretty fucking sound. "Ahhh—God. Yes, Killian," she cries out as shudders rack her beautiful body, and her tight, hot, cunt squeezes the life out of me.

I slow my thrusts, fucking her through her orgasm, dragging it out until she whimpers, "It's too much."

And when I lay her back down against the bed, limp and sated, I keep her legs wrapped around my hips, fucking her slowly.

My eyes stay glued to her breasts, swaying with each snap of my hips.

This . . . I think . . . this was the picture I've imagined the most over the years.

A sex-drunk, sexy smile pulls at her beautiful lips. "Killian," she keens, and I swear to God, I could come just from the way she says my damn name. "I can't come again. I've never—"

Needing to be deeper, and refusing to accept that she can't, I cup her ass in my hands and drive into her depths.

This was how it was always supposed to be.

Lilah comes back to me, whimpering, and I set a punishing rhythm, fucking away all the hate until there's just us.

Just here and now.

Until she's right here with me again, begging.

My muscles contract with every snap of my hips against hers, every drip of Lilah's soaked cunt sliding around my dick. Every moan and whimper and scream.

White-hot sizzling heat licks down the base of my spine as a towering inferno devours us both, and we fuck our way through all the pain.

Lilah

Chapter 15

My mom once told me the French don't say "I miss you."
They say, "tu me manques" which translates to "you are
missing from me." I didn't understand the difference
before. I do now.

—*Lilah's Secret Thoughts*

"You should probably answer that." Killian buries his face in my neck and pulls my naked body back against his, making it hard to think.

"I don't want to." I'm definitely pouting, but after nearly thirty-six hours wrapped up in this man, I'm not ready for our bubble to burst and for things to go back to the way they were. It's getting harder to remember why they have to with each new hour and each new orgasm.

His lips press against the top of my spine, and I feel it down to the tips of my toes. "They've been calling for five minutes, princess. It might be important."

I grab the phone from the nightstand and roll over to face him, absolutely loving the way his eyes grow wide like he hasn't spent the last day and a half worshipping my body. "Hello?"

Killian sucks my nipple into his mouth, and I gasp.

"Lilah?" Scottie asks with concern in her voice. "Are you okay? I've been trying to reach you. You sound out of breath."

"Sorry . . . sorry," I laugh to hide my moan and fail epically. "I was just . . . uh . . . stepping into the tub. The hot water feels heavenly."

Killian switches to the other breast and drags his teeth over my nipple, making me hiss.

Shit.

I swat at his head but don't move even an inch away.

"Sure. All right." No way she actually believed that. "Well, I spoke to Iris this morning, and she had some good news. They secured insurance for the tour, and they're ready to talk dates."

Shit.

"Already?" I pull back and sit up, immediately missing our connection. "When?"

"Three weeks."

"No. It can't be that soon." I pull the sheet up around my chest and lean back against the headboard, watching Killian as he props himself up on his elbow, glued to my every word. "Killian's fight is in two months. I'll get you an exact date, but I don't want to pick it back up until after the fight."

Killian's green eyes narrow and harden setting me on edge.

"Iris isn't going to like this," Scottie warns, but I'm over caring. "Neither is Zoe."

"Seems like these days, if I'm not pissing off Iris, I'm pissing off Zoe. Guess I better get comfortable with unhappy people if it makes me happy."

"What's Zoe pissed about?"

I look down at Killian, not really wanting him to hear this

but not having much choice. "She sent me a message. She wasn't thrilled with the way Killian and I went public at my birthday party."

"Yeah . . . I guess she wasn't ready for that." I know Scottie says something else, but I've stopped listening as I watch Killian climb out of bed, clearly pissed. Damn it.

"Scottie . . ." She keeps talking, but now Killian's throwing on jeans, and I feel like I'm about to lose something I might not get back. "Scottie—" I nearly shout. "I've got to go. Tell Iris not until after the fight. We'll talk more tomorrow."

"Lilah—"

"Bye." I disconnect the call and jump out of bed, completely naked, and throw on Killian's Crucible t-shirt from the end of the bed. "Kill . . . stop. I'm sorry."

He zips his jeans and leaves them hanging unbuttoned on his hips. "Did they even talk safety protocols with you?"

"What?" Acid churns in my stomach. He sounds so angry. "Protocols? You heard what I said. We were talking scheduling. But if you don't want me at your fight, I don't have to be there."

"Lilah Belle." His deep voice softens as he reaches for me, but I back away, already shutting down. I can't handle his rejection if that's what he's giving me. Not now. Not again. "The only thing I care about is your safety. You didn't even ask about it. Some psycho is stalking you. He tried to kill you and nearly took half a damn stadium out in the process, and you didn't even ask about safety or what they're doing to keep you safe. You just started talking dates, like it's a done deal."

"Killian . . ." Shit. He's not rejecting me. He's scared. "I didn't ask because I'm not the one who handles that stuff. I let the experts deal with the safety, and I don't interfere, just like I wouldn't take their advice on how I should sing."

"How can you be so unconcerned with your own life, Lilah?"

"I'm not unconcerned. I just trust my team," I snap but then walk into his chest and wrap my arms around his waist. "I don't tell you how to fight. You can't tell me how to run my tour."

He kisses the top of my head. "Sounds like someone has to, princess."

What the fuck?

I pull back, officially pissed. This is what I get for being comfortable. "I'm sorry. Do you think fucking me for two days gives you the right to tell me how to run my business?"

"This isn't your business, Lilah. It's your life," he yells. "This man is stalking you."

I tilt my head and look at the gorgeous man in front of me and play his words over in my head. "That's the second time you used that word." My throat gets dry as something clicks in place . . . followed by a hit of denial. "I don't have a stalker."

"Yeah, you fucking do." He closes the distance between us and cups my face in his hands.

He's too close, and I can't think.

I can't rationalize what he's saying.

"No. I don't. *But* . . . "I'd know if I did."

"Yes, you do." His thumbs strokes my jaw, and I feel like I'm hearing everything in a tunnel as cars fly by. "Everyone's so worried about upsetting you and protecting you, they don't even realize that by hiding it, they're putting you at risk. Fuck, Lilah, nothing scares me, but I'm scared for you."

His words start to slowly sink in.

A stalker.

The bomb . . .

"How long?" My voice is barely a whisper, and when Killian's face sinks, I feel crushed. "Killian . . ."

"I don't know. Noah didn't tell me how long."

"What?" The scared whisper is gone, replaced by loud and shrill and pissed off. "Noah knows?"

When Killian doesn't answer me, I push back against his chest and out of his hold. "Who else?" I demand and storm over to my closet and grab a pair of jeans. "Who else knows, Killian? Do my parents?"

His face blanches, and I want to scream.

Oh, you've got to be kidding me.

I throw on my jeans, stuff my feet into Uggs, and take a deep breath that does nothing to calm me down or clear the storm. "Can you please drive me to my parents' house? I really don't want Xander there for my messy family drama."

"They're trying to protect you, Lilah. That's all any of us are trying to do."

"You don't get to make that call. None of you do. I get to decide. And I can't do that if I don't have all the facts. Now either come with me to my parents' house or don't, and I'll go by myself. But I'm leaving, so you better decide now." I don't know who I'm more upset with . . . Everyone who's kept this from me by making decisions about my life without including me in the process or myself for letting them.

"*D*amn it." Cars line my parents' driveway. More cars than I was expecting.

"Looks like your whole family's here," Killian murmurs as we pull in behind Addie and Leo's car. It's the first words we've spoken since we left my house. I'm not even sure if I'm mad at him or at everyone else and Killian is just being lumped in with them.

I don't answer before I throw open the door with the raging strength of a woman pissed on a visceral level. No one can hurt you more than the people you love.

"Lilah," he calls out as I pass more cars, marching toward the door.

I don't knock.

They're already expecting me, even if they have no clue how pissed I am.

Guess they're about to find out.

Killian catches up to me and takes my hand in his before I can rip it away. When I try to pull away, he refuses to let go. "Lilah," he warns, softly. "Don't do this. Talk to them when you're not so raw."

"No." I yank my hand from his and spin around right into my grandfather's arms.

"Lilah Belle. My girl. Happy birthday."

"Hi, Grandpa." I kiss his cheek and hold myself there for a minute, soaking in his love. He's been battling cancer for months, but he looks better than the last time I saw him. Hopefully, that's a good sign.

His dark brows furrow. "You okay, sweetheart?"

"I need to find Mom and Dad. Are they in the kitchen?" My voice shakes, and he doesn't miss the tell. *Shit.*

"Hey, Tink," Asher walks by and fist-bumps Killian. "Mom's looking for you. She's in the kitchen."

"Excuse me." I don't stop for anyone else. Not the entire fleet of kids my cousins have that are running circles around Jamie. Not for Dillan or Addie. Not until I see Noah fingering the icing on his heart-shaped cake while Mom sips a giant cup of coffee. "You asshole," I yell the second I'm standing across from him, and the chatter in the room stops. My loud, obnoxious family, silent for one of the first times in recent history.

"What the hell?" Noah looks at me like I've suddenly

grown horns and a tale. "Dude. Whatever it is, I didn't do it." He smirks, jokingly, then looks beside me. "Killian did."

"Wrong fucking answer." I somehow manage to keep my voice steady as my veins pump in double time to keep up with the blood boiling in my veins "You told Killian I have a stalker."

"You have a stalker?" Asher asks from behind me, and I'm pretty sure Dillan covers his mouth.

"What the hell, man?" Noah narrows his eyes on Killian, like he's the problem. "I trusted you not to say anything."

"Are you serious right now?" I move in front of Killian, keeping my brother's attention on me. "You don't get to be mad that he told me something about *my* life. *My* life, Noah. How could you keep that from me? How could you not demand I be told?" I slap my hand against the marble countertop and ignore the sting that shoots up my arm. "How many other people know? Who else did you trust enough to make decisions about my life?"

"Noah." Mom's voice is shaking, and when I look over at her, it's clear as day on her face. She didn't know. "Is this true?"

"They said it was safer for her this way," Noah argues as my father walks into the room.

His eyes are wide as he takes in the tension in the room. "What the hell is going on in here?"

"Oh, you'd have to ask Noah that, Daddy. See, he decided he knew best, so now he's the only one in this room who knows anything." Tears threaten to spring free as my anger reaches new levels I didn't know I was capable of. "How could you?"

"Tink—" He moves toward me, and Killian reaches around my waist and holds me back when he realizes I'm about to launch myself at Noah.

"Don't you fucking dare. A stalker? You kept a stalker

from me. How long?" I'm not even sure I'm making sense, and I'm less sure I care. "How long did you know some sicko was stalking me and that they were the one who sent the bomb that almost killed me, Noah?"

"Okay. That's it," Dad stops me—well, he tries to. But I'm done.

"No answer, huh, Noah? Well, fuck you. I never would have done this to you. Never would have kept this from you." My entire body vibrates with fury, and I realize Killian is still holding me back.

"I was trying to keep you safe, Tink," Noah yells back at me, and I lose it.

"Yeah well, I'm not your job anymore, Noah. They secured the insurance for the rest of the tour. I'm going back out, and you're not going with me. You're fired."

"Lilah—" Mom gasps, but I ignore her and the way she reaches for Dad.

"I'm calling a meeting with my agent and the label tomorrow." I look between my parents, ignoring Noah and every other family member who's in the room. "Once I get all the details, I'll fill you both in. But I am going back on tour. I'm not letting a stalker or anyone else dictate my life for me." I look over my shoulder at Killian, who's still got me anchored to him. "I'd like to go now."

"Lilah, please . . ." Noah pleads, but I shake my head. "I'm sorry."

"No. We've always been equals . . . until now. I've always included you in decisions. But you chose not to. I'm not sure what you were thinking, but you don't get to unilaterally make a decision about my life. Looks like since you did, now I am too." My breath catches in my chest, but I refuse to cry. Not in front of everyone. Not even my family.

I've spent a decade fighting to be taken seriously.

To not be treated like some little girl.

To own my own career.

And in one night, I feel like that was taken away from me.

A lifetime of work.

Of sacrifice.

Gone.

Killian

Chapter 16

ilah refuses to look at or speak to me on the drive home. She walks silently into the house and up the stairs, and the quiet closing of her bedroom door is louder than any slamming could ever be. She's hurting, and I don't know how to help her.

I'm not sure how long I stand at the bottom of the stairs before my phone vibrates in my pocket. Fucking hell. Don't let this be Noah.

I don't need to be any more in the middle of this shit show than I already am.

JAMIE
Is she okay?

KILLIAN
Did she look okay to you?

JAMIE
None of that was okay.

KILLIAN
She's in her room. I'm giving her space.

JAMIE

Don't give her too much space. You know she'll shut down.

Don't I fucking know it.

That's Lilah's MO.

She has the biggest heart of anyone I've ever known. But damn, if you hurt her, she can shut you out and not look back. I don't think she'll do that to Noah, but I didn't think she'd do it to me, and look at us now. None of this is going to be easily dealt with.

KILLIAN

Yeah. I got it.

JAMIE

May the force be with you.

KILLIAN

You're still fucking weird, dude.

JAMIE

Yoda was the man, asshole.

KILLIAN

Whatever you have to tell yourself.

I think about going down to the gym to work out but take the stairs up two at a time instead. I raise my hand to knock on the door but stop when I hear her crying, and my heart cracks. In all the years I've known this woman, I've only ever seen her cry once. And that time, it was my fault.

"Lilah," I call through the door.

"Go away, Killian," she yells through her tears.

"Can't do that, princess." I wrap my hand around the doorknob but wait. "I'm worried about you."

"Why?" Her voice sounds closer. "You don't even like me." She sounds like she's on the other side of the door.

"You know that's not true." The knob turns in my hand, but I'm not the one turning it. When the door opens, her face is red, and her wild blonde hair is sticking to her cheeks. She's stripped out of her jeans, but she's still wearing my Crucible t-shirt and a pair of fuzzy socks. She's the most stunningly beautiful mess I've ever seen in my life.

"I feel like I don't know anything right now." Thick tears cling to her long lashes, and I wipe them away with my thumbs.

"I get that, and I'm sorry if I played a part in this. I do think Noah meant well, but—"

"Don't." She shakes her head. "Don't defend him."

Lilah walks back over to her bed and crawls under the blanket. "I just want to forget this day ever happened."

I want to remind her that the first half of the day was pretty fucking spectacular, but even I'm not that big of an asshole. But I follow her over anyway and climb in bed behind her, then pull her to me. "Sleep, princess. It might all look different in the morning."

She doesn't say anything, but the slight shake of her body from her silent tears eventually stops, and her breathing evens out. All the while, she holds the arm I have wrapped around her like it's her security blanket. And with nothing but time to watch her sleep in the silence of the night, a few things become crystal clear.

I'm not sure when I fall asleep, but when I wake up, the moon is reflecting off the snow, giving a silvery glow to everything inside Lilah's bedroom. Everything but her—because she's not here. I worry for a quick second before the soothing sound of the piano breaks through my sleep-deprived brain.

Guess that answers where she is.

I follow the sound down, and when I hit the bottom of the stairs, I can make out her voice too. She's quiet, but man, her voice has always been the only thing in the world as beautiful as she is.

When I find her, she's sitting at her black, baby-grand piano in the dark room, lit only by a single candle and the snow falling outside, shining through the three walls of floor-to-ceiling windows. The melody is heartbreaking, but watching her play it while she works out the words she wants is fascinating.

"Did anyone ever tell you it's rude to eavesdrop?" She's asking me a question but still running her fingers over the keys.

"I may have been told that a time or two, but I was never good at following the rules." I don't move from the edge of the room, trying to let her have her space if that's what she wants. What she needs. It's not what I want, but this isn't about me.

"What are you doing out of bed, champ?"

"Just checking on you." I cross my arms over my chest, and Lilah tracks the movement. Her expressive eyes showing every thought she's thinking. And there's a whole lot going on there. "You want me to leave you alone?"

"What are you doing, Killian?" Her fingers stop playing, and she places them in her lap.

"Didn't we just do this?" I'm playing dumb, hoping like

hell she's not trying to pick a fight but knowing this woman well enough to know that's exactly what she's doing.

"I mean what are you doing here? With me? Why did you agree to this whole thing? We don't even like each other. Why were you willing to help me in the first place?" She fires her questions off rapid-paced, but I don't budge. Don't falter. Don't hesitate. Because to Lilah, any of those things would be a betrayal.

"You know you ask a whole lotta questions, but you don't want to give me any time to answer. I bet you *think* you already know the answers. But you're wrong," I challenge her because this . . . this kind of banter, this is where we shine.

"Cite your source," she counters.

"I'm my own source, princess. You want to know why I'm here? Well, the answer to that one question answers all your little follow-ups too, so buckle up, buttercup. Because you're not going to like this." Her cheeks flame red, and she looks so fucking beautiful, I have to force myself to stay put and not just give in and go to her. We've been here before, and it didn't go so well for us then.

"I'm here because it's you, Lilah. You and me. I'm here because it's always been you and me. Always. Even when you said you hated me. Even when you swore I hated you. Even when you told me you never wanted to speak to me again, it was still you and me. I will always be here for you. I will always protect you. I will always lo—"

"Don't you dare finish that sentence. I can't— My God, I can't do this. Not now. I can't go there. I can't dredge that all up and expect to come out the other side okay. I don't have the emotional capacity to handle any more at this point today." She runs her fingers lovingly along the white keys as if grounding herself, and I'm not even sure she realizes she's doing it. "I already cut my brother out today. The only person I trusted completely. It used to be you and him and then it was just him . . . And now—just don't, Killian. I can't handle it tonight . . . Please."

I bite my tongue. I don't throw in her face that she asked in the first place. "Okay. Not tonight. But we're going to discuss this at some point."

Fuck.

I hate being the one to walk away, but that's what she's asking.

She wants me to leave her alone with her music.

It's how she processes the world.

"We really don't have to. I won't ask again." She picks her notebook up from the piano and jots something down.

"You won't have to. I will," I promise, then walk away.

149

Lilah

Chapter 17

If the shoe fits, strut your stuff, Cinderella.

—*Lilah's Secret Thoughts*

*L*ennox snuggles her sweet-smelling head into the crook of my neck and yawns.

Me too, baby girl. Me too.

Meanwhile, her momma's eyes might as well be drilling a hole into the side of my head from the other end of my couch as she waits for an answer I don't know if I'm ready to give.

"Can you repeat the question?" I stall, and Addie just shakes her head.

"Lilah Belle Ryan," she calls me out.

"Okay, first, you've been around the family way too much if you're using my full name." I lower my voice and pat Lennox's tiny tush when she startles against me. "Fine . . ." I whisper-hiss. "No. I haven't spoken to Noah. I met with my manager and the label last week and lost my mind when they told me everything that has been sent by '*With all my love.*' That's how this sicko has been signing everything."

"Creepy much? My God, Lilah. How long has it been going on?"

"I've gotten weird things before, but they think this one started early last year. But they only started escalating and signing their messages two-ish months ago." A chill rips down my back, and I close my eyes, hating how vulnerable this makes me feel.

Addie looks distraught, and I wonder how it's been just a few months since I met her when it feels like years. "Has Noah known the whole time?"

I shake my head, and my heart sinks. "He found out recently. But it doesn't matter. He still kept it from me. God, Addie. I'm so mad at him . . . I've never been this mad at him before."

"Have you talked to him?"

I shrug. "Sort of, but not really." I try to push away the hurt, but it doesn't work. "We've texted. He's checked in to see if I'm okay. If I'm safe. But we haven't really talked, and we haven't discussed the tour. Not yet. I know we need to, but I think about it, and I just get so freaking upset all over again."

"Did you tell the label you fired him?" She looks at me over the top of her coffee cup, and I think if she could have backed away as she asked the question, she would have. I get the feeling everyone in my life is bracing for the impact that Noah and I fighting will have on everything. Like they know the blast zone will be enormous.

"No, I didn't tell them I fired him. I just told them I wouldn't start the tour until after Killian's fight. That gives me a few more weeks to either calm down or not. It's not like I can fire my entire team, and I'm under contract with the label. So, I'm basically stuck surrounded by people I can no longer trust, and I just don't know what the hell I'm supposed to do with that."

"Oh, babe, I'm so sorry." She pulls a cookie from the pink Sweet Temptations bag between us and offers it to me. "You could use this more than me."

"I will never turn down a chocolate chip cookie." With zero hesitation, I snatch that sucker out of her hand. "I swear these are better than sex."

Addie chokes on her coffee as I pop the rest in my mouth.

"I'm sorry, but you must be doing it wrong, if that's true."

I think about Killian.

His weight on my body.

His hands on my hips.

His lips on mine.

Him . . . Why the hell is it always him?

"Or maybe you do know what you're doing." She points at my face, and I bite down on my lip as my cheeks flame red.

"It's complicated," I offer, not sure I want to open Pandora's box. Not when Pandora and I have barely spoken in the week since we blew up.

"Dumb it down for me and take your time. I've got four hours before I have to pick up Izzy."

"Dumb it down . . . I'm not sure how to do that." Even as I admit that, I know it'll never appease Addie.

She tilts her head and drops it to the hand cocked against the back of the couch. "Listen to me, okay? Your drama couldn't be worse than mine, could it? Your cousin spent a night in jail for me."

"Ours is different," I muse softly, and she yawns. "Fine. Point taken, but if you turn this into a book, we're no longer friends."

Her warm smile stretches across her face, and I sip my tea, not sure I'm ready to go back there. How much drama can one person handle in a week?

"We were kids. Kids playing at being adults. Sixteen years

old when it went to hell in a perfectly wrapped package. But that's not how it started. We were inseparable growing up."

"But you didn't grow up in Kroydon Hills, did you?"

"I spent a few months here every year. Every spring and summer before football season started. You know my dad and Jamie's dad both played football for Baltimore, so that lasted until they retired." I warm, remembering how much I looked forward to coming back here each year. Wanting Dad to make the playoffs but also desperate for the season to end because the kids here were different from the ones we knew there. "Once he retired, that was it. We were back full-time, and everything changed. Uncle Murphy retired the next year, and by sixth grade, Noah, Jamie, Maverick, Killian, and I were all in the same grade, and we were our own little impenetrable clique. The girls in my class either hated me because I was friends with the guys or tried to be my friend just so they could get close to them. They'd ditch me when they realized the guys weren't interested. At least, not until high school."

"Okay . . . I can see that. Little bitches. I'm dreading when my girls are old enough to deal with the mean girls."

"Yeah, it sucked. But I had the guys, and I had my music, and that was all I needed." I think back to the innocence of those few years when the worst thing in the world was having your cell phone taken away as punishment or being grounded for a weekend. As we got older, innocence and freedom started to give way to hormones and other interests, like music and sports. "All I needed *until* I wanted more."

"Okay." She tucks her legs up under herself. "Now we're getting somewhere. I want to hear about the hormones and waning innocence."

"Oh, good grief, you little romance writer. Always down for the drama," I poke, and she smiles.

"Yup. Now stop *stalling*. Again."

"You've got to understand . . . by the time I was sixteen, I felt like I was twenty-six. My parents were the absolute opposite of stage parents. But they supported my dreams and helped me achieve them. But doing that meant working hard. Performing. Practicing. Writing songs. I felt like school was a part-time job before I officially dropped out for my first tour."

"Did whatever the hell happened happen before or after you left for your tour?"

"Before," I whisper.

The weekend before.

"<big>*W*</big>*hy don't you want to go to Gia's party tonight?"* Seventeen-year-old Killian asks me from behind a heavy bag hanging in Crucible. Seventeen. How does he possibly look like this at seventeen? Even Jamie and Maverick don't have the muscles Killian has, and they're both looking at D1 football scholarships for college. The gym is basically a dead zone because of the snowstorm raging outside. Meanwhile, I'm a hot mess from the emotions I've got raging inside.*

Maybe that's why I don't feel like going to a house party overflowing with beer, sports bros, and bitchy girls. Okay, and maybe I just wanted to soak up as much alone time with Killian as I can before I leave for the tour.

"I don't know." I shrug and go back to doodling on the dotted page in front of me. "I guess I don't want to spend one of my last nights home with all the catty girls from high school staring at me with daggers in their eyes because they think I'm the reason you won't date them."

"Listen, if they can't handle the truth, that's on them." He throws a punch against the bag, and I feel it in my chest.

"What?" I close my favorite pink notebook with the tiny white strawberry blossoms on the cover and tuck my pen inside so I can give him my full attention while my mind runs rampant with possibilities. "What—what truth?"

Killian stops the momentum of the bag with his hands, then moves until he's standing in front of me, his toes touching mine as he looks down at me. Knees bent and back against the wall, I tilt my face all the way up to him and smile. "What are you talking about, champ?"

He reaches a hand out to me and waits for me to take it.

So damn confident because he's pulled me up from this floor a million times.

So many hours of writing while he spars.

So it's no surprise when I slide my hand in his and let him pull me to my feet. But the look on his face is different this time. It's confusing and exciting and makes it hard to breathe.

"The truth, princess. The one they all know but you don't." His rough thumb traces circles on my wrist, and I want to squirm under his touch, but I don't. This is Killian. The boy who carried my books for me for weeks when I was stuck in an air boot freshman year. The one who never misses a performance. The one who gave me my lucky necklace.

"Help me out then. It's not nice that I'm the only one left in the dark." I smile and hold my ground.

This moment feels important.

Or maybe that's just my inner romantic running wild.

"The one where they know they can't hold a candle to you, Lilah Belle."

Oh . . . that.

"Right. Because I'm your best friend and all . . ."

Not like I haven't heard that before.

Broken. Record.

Killian wraps a big hand around the back of my head in a way he's never touched me before, and I think my heart skips a beat. "No, Lilah. Because it's you . . . And you're—you're different."

He tilts my head back, so I'm looking right into his bright green eyes, and I realize I only have a few days left before I leave. That's the only reason I grow the lady balls I suddenly have. "Are you ever going to kiss me, Killian?"

"Lilah . . ." He swallows, and I think my heart sinks down to the floor with that one movement.

"Oh my goodness . . . I shouldn't have—I didn't mean—" I pull back, but Killian's hold on me tightens.

"Just wait, princess. Not all of us have the same way with words you do. It takes some of us longer to put our thoughts together." His lips tug up, and I want to cry.

I don't want to leave him.

Everything is going to be different when I come back.

But I have to go.

This is my dream.

"Lilah . . . I'm not going to kiss you tonight because you leave in five days, twelve hours, and"—he looks over at the clock then back to me and blows out his breath—"and about forty-five minutes."

"What does that have to do with anything?" My defenses go up, and my confusion settles in for another round of ping-pong.

"Because when I kiss you, Lilah, it's going to be the beginning of everything, not the end. It's not going to be goodbye. It's going to be welcome home, I missed you." I gasp, and Killian takes a step impossibly closer, sucking every last little bit of oxygen from the gym, making it hard to breathe.

"When I kiss you, you're going to be the last girl I kiss for the rest of my life. It was always going to be you. You're it. You're going to be my girl. And I'm not ready for that with you leaving. Your life is about to explode, and I can't wait to watch it all happen for you, but I'm not going to be the asshole who makes you wish you were here instead of doing your thing. The whole world is going to fall in

love with you, Lilah, and I'm a greedy asshole who wishes he didn't have to share you already."

"Killian . . ." I whisper as the first tear falls.

"No tears, princess. I'm going to need you to remember that I loved you first, and when you're done, I'm going to love you last. Can you do that for me?"

"What if I don't want to wait?" I ask so softly, I'm surprised he can even hear me.

The way he runs his hand over my head sends tingles through my entire body.

"Guess you're going to have to trust me." He pulls me against his chest, and I wrap my arms around his waist. "Do you trust me, Lilah?"

"With my life, Killian."

"Then trust that we don't have to rush the start when the good stuff is going to last us till we're old and gray and pissing off your brother with the way I still can't keep my hands off you. Trust us to know when it's right. You're on tour for ten months . . ."

My heart is breaking in my chest.

Cracking in half and shattering.

"I could come home between cities—"

"No, you can't. That's exactly what you can't do. Give this tour everything it deserves. You've worked your perfect ass off for this forever. Find me when you come home. I'll still be right here."

"And you'll be mine?" I breathe out, terrified that we're never going to get this moment back.

"I've always been yours."

"Oh. My. God. How did you go from that to hating him?" Addie asks through a sniffle, pulling me out of the memory, and I wipe my tear-stained cheeks.

Damn it. This is why I don't go back there. I can't.

I push it all back down into that little box and shove it to the deepest recesses of my brain. "And then he showered, and we went to Gia Petrillo's party where I caught Killian and Gia fucking against the pool house."

"Shut up," she all but screams, and Lennox whines and shifts.

"Nope." I shake my head slowly, forcing myself not to relive the pain. "I saw it and left, and the next day, we got into a huge fight." I stand with the baby in my arms and sway, hoping it will calm both of us down. "It went downhill from there."

"Well hell, Lilah. You guys have never talked about it since?"

I shake my head, wishing there was a different answer. Hell, she watches me like she's expecting a different answer. Like there's going to be some misunderstanding that's going to make it all better. But there's not. "I cried every day for a month, but it didn't change anything."

I wish it had.

SCOTTIE

Iris confirmed the tour dates.

LILAH

And?

SCOTTIE

First stop is the Wednesday after the fight.

LILAH

How long will I be gone?

SCOTTIE

Seven weeks. With breaks in-between. You could fly home a few times if you want to.

LILAH

Okay.

SCOTTIE

You gonna tell me we need a new band leader?

LILAH

Why? What did you hear and from who?

SCOTTIE

A lady never reveals her sources.

LILAH

Good thing I'm not talking to a lady then.

SCOTTIE

Hey!

LILAH

You're a shark, and you know it. And I haven't decided on the band leader yet. It's still to be determined.

SCOTTIE

Seven weeks isn't a ton of time to find a replacement.

LILAH

I know.

SCOTTIE

I'll put feelers out without making too much noise.

LILAH

Thanks.

SCOTTIE

He was trying to protect you, Lilah.

LILAH

Yeah. So were you, and I haven't forgiven you yet either. I have to love him. I don't even have to like you. So drop it.

The Philly Press

CUPIDS ARROW MISSED AGAIN

Rumor has it Kroydon Hills newest *It* Couple, Lilah Ryan and Killian St. James, seem to have already hit a rough road. With news spreading that the *Captivating* tour will be kicking back off shortly, will they be able to navigate two high-profile careers on opposite ends of the world or could this be another instance of Cupid's arrow wearing off a little too soon? Our source says this MMA prince tried to buy everyone's favorite pop princess's affection with a certain gift that's still sitting in the box. Brr. Sounds like things are cooling down to me.

#KroydonKronicles #Prince&Princess
#CupidsArrowMissedAgain

Killian

Chapter 18

"*R*emind me why I'm here when I could still be in bed with a hot redhead?" Rome grunts as he brings his knee up but misses when I sidestep. The fucker stumbles, and I smile.

"Because you're a twisted fuck who loves to fight," Hudson yells from outside the cage. "Now shut up and focus."

The psycho salutes, and I tune out whatever Hudson and Dad say when I see my chance.

Sloppy asshole.

I grab his arm and drop to my back.

We learned arm bars twenty years ago, and this dumb ass still didn't see it coming.

"Tap, asshole," I growl while I squeeze my legs around him, hips off the floor, and his arm hyperextended.

Tight.

Tighter.

"Tap."

"Never," he wheezes.

Tighter.

"Fuck, no."

I lock him down, my muscles screaming from the exertion, and he finally gives in seconds before we both roll flat, starfishing against the mats.

"Goddamn, I hate you," Rome bitches as he tests out his shoulder, making sure I didn't pop it out. I didn't. Big fucking baby.

I bridge up and jump to my feet, then pull him up too. "Told you to tap."

We walk over to Hudson and Dad, who are both smiling for a change. "Good effort today, guys." Dad crosses his arms and waits for us to climb down the steps. "We've got some news."

"Oh yeah?" I have no idea where he's going with this, but he's smiling, and he rarely smiles during training. Then I realize he's not smiling at me.

"You think you're ready, Rome?"

"Ready?" My typically cocky cousin has a moment of hesitation before his crazy kicks in. "No fucking way. I've got a fight?"

Damn. He's worked his ass off for this for years.

"Welterweight in Atlantic City in April." Dad smacks his back. "You earned it, kid."

"Fucking right, I did. Now, let's go celebrate."

"Celebrate after you win, psycho." Hudson points between us. "Wins are built in the gym. You've got two hours of conditioning left."

Rome rubs his hand together like a cartoon villain. "I vote for conditioning at Lilah's house."

"I don't want to know. Just get it done," Dad tells us before he walks away.

Hudson, however, looks intrigued. "Do I want to know?"

Rome bounces on the balls of his feet with excitement. "Dude. I heard a rumor Dillan's been at her house, helping her with shit lately. Have you seen Dillan Ryan's ass? I'd tap that in a heartbeat."

"Jesus Christ, you're fucking lucky people are scared of your dad, or you'd be dead already," Hudson grumbles.

"They should be more scared of Mom," Rome corrects him, and I shove his back.

"Stay the fuck away from Dillan. There's a ton of shit going on in that family right now. They don't need your brand of trouble too."

"Does that go for you too, Killer?" The look Hudson gives me tells me he already knows the answer, but the dick asks anyway.

"Nobody told me to stay away." I pull the wraps from my hand and shove them into my pockets, then grab a towel.

"Walk with me, kid." Hudson doesn't wait for an answer because it wasn't a question. He crosses the mats and heads upstairs to the yoga studio Dad installed a few years ago and starts cleaning up what was tossed aside after the sunrise class earlier. "Have you given any thought to what comes after this next fight?"

"One fight at a time, Uncle. You know the rules." Truth is, I haven't. It's been a struggle just to stay focused on the fight in front of me with everything else that's been going on.

"You're twenty-six, Killer. You need to start thinking about what comes next, and I wouldn't be doing my job if I didn't point that out. Rome's fighting welterweight this year, but if he bulks up like he wants to, he's going to be heavyweight real soon. You've got a few years left of this, if you're lucky and stay healthy. I need you to start thinking ahead. By the time I was your age, Sawyer and I were already establishing our real estate venture. Because, believe it or not, you're not going to want to put your body through this forever."

It feels like he just dropped a ten-ton bomb in my lap, and I'm staring at one blue cord and one red one, trying to decide which to cut to stop time from ticking down. "I'm twenty-six, not forty-six. I've got time."

"It feels like that today. But that switch is going to flip fast, Killer. I just want you to be prepared when it does. It might be ten years from now, or it could be ten months from now. Start thinking about it. Start making plans, even if you don't tell a soul. At least you'll have ideas." He hands me an empty water bottle. "And keep an eye on Rome for me. I swear he's gonna get himself killed."

"Yeah well, if he fucks around with Dillan, I'll do it myself." Damn, Lilah would be so pissed.

"I always thought you had a thing for the other Ryan sister." He knows I do. *Asshole.* "Yeah, that's what I thought. Might want to get your house in order, Killian. Pretty women with brains and confidence don't like to be dicked around."

"Nobody's getting dicked around." I fail to mention that's because we've barely spoken since her birthday and everything that came after. She comes with me here every morning and leaves with Xander every afternoon. She's basically become a shut-in, and it feels wrong. Like she's become a prisoner in her own world, and I don't know how the hell to help her.

"Whatever you say," Hudson taunts. "Are you bringing Lilah to the Kingston Foundation event, or are you flying solo?"

When I don't answer him, he curses. "Listen up, nephew. You've got way too many moving pieces in your life to be getting ready for a fight next month. Get it together. Claim the girl or don't. Make plans for a life after fighting or fight until you've got a walker. I don't care either way. I just want to see you happy, and I gotta tell you, I don't think you are. Figure it out."

He walks away, and I'm left standing, unbalanced, like I

just took a roundhouse kick to the skull. What the fuck? I'm happy. I live a fucking fantastic life.

I do what I want.

When I want.

I'm the goddamned heavyweight champion.

I work hard, enjoy my life, and—

And what?

Lilah's beautiful face flashes in front of me.

And what . . . ?

And it can all go away in the blink of an eye.

Fuck. I hate when he's right.

Get my house in order.

It's time.

$\mathcal{M}$y stomach growls as I walk into Lilah's later that afternoon. The scent of garlic and onions and tomatoes wafts through the house, followed by little girl giggles.

"You gotta put salt in the water, Aunt Tink."

"Fuck, our girl can cook too?" Rome smacks my chest and pushes past me, on a mission for the kitchen, and I yank him back by his shirt.

"My girl, you stupid son of a bitch."

The crazy shit's smile stretches across his whole face. There's a reason he's been called a psycho since he was a kid. And that smile is the reason. "Took you long enough, Killer."

"She can't cook. That smell and that voice means Maverick's here," I tell him as I push him behind me.

"No shit, dumbass. That smell is Nonna's sauce, and only a few of us have that recipe. Now get out of my way. I don't have to watch weight for my fight yet, and I'm starving."

"We've got to do conditioning," I warn him while my stomach tries to eat itself.

Damn, that smells so good.

"Food first. Condition after."

I let him go and follow him into the kitchen, where Mav, Lilah, and Dillan are following Rosie's instructions on how to make the perfect pasta.

"Ladies." Rome salutes before he walks over to the sink and washes his hands, then shows them to Rosie for inspection. "Look. No peanut butter."

She smiles and nods, then reaches her arms up for a hug.

"I keep telling you it's gross, Rome."

He sits her on his hip and laughs. "I know, but I love it."

"Did you eat it today?" She asks and smiles when he tells her no, then kisses his cheek.

But it's not Rosie's smile that could knock me over.

It's Lilah's.

It's the way she watches the interaction. With longing. Though I'm not sure for what.

Maverick grabs the plates from the cabinet like it's his house. "You two eating dinner?"

"Yes," Rome answers as I say, "No."

"Aww, don't be a party pooper, Killer," Dillan teases as she places a wooden salad bowl on the kitchen table. "Rosie just taught us how to make Nonna's sauce."

When my eyes find Lilah's, so damn soft and hesitant, it just about kills me.

Like she wants something, but she's scared to ask for it.

"Yeah, champ. Don't be a party pooper," she whispers, and I'm done for. It's the closest she's come to asking me for anything since she asked me to protect her.

"Okay," I give in and watch Lilah's teeth graze over her lip in an attempt to hide her smile. "But I think Rome should have to do the dishes."

"What?" he sputters. "Why me?"

"Yup," I steal Rosie from him and kiss the top of her head.

"Because we cooked," Maverick hands Rome the plates and grabs a pitcher of water.

"Killian didn't cook," he argues.

"Killian lives here," Lilah says softly. "He gets a pass. Now eat before it gets cold."

I look over the top of Rosie's head at this woman who never stops surprising me, but she looks away.

Yeah . . . It's long past time I do something about this.

*T*here's a knock about working out in Lilah's gym. Knowing she's upstairs.

In one way, it's a good thing. I know she's safe.

In another way, it's torture—because I know she's upstairs.

Mav and Rosie stuck around until Rosie started yawning.

Rome and Dillan left separately just after that.

Not that Rome didn't try to leave together, but Dillan shot that shit down.

It was epic.

It was also good for me. I don't need Rome for conditioning. I've never needed anyone to tell me to get it done. It's part of the job, and it's part of what makes me the best. What made it hard to keep going tonight was the piano playing that replaced my normal playlist because once I heard it, there was no way I was putting my headphones on. Not when I could listen to that . . . to her instead.

And once I'm finally done, it takes all my strength to leave Lilah alone.

I force myself to go up to my room and shower.

I don't interrupt her.

I don't want to fuck with her process.

Not when it sounds like it's working.

Instead, I pull out my phone and pull up my text thread, then let my thumb hover over Noah's name with Maddox's advice from weeks ago stuck in my mind.

KILLIAN

I'm in love with your sister.

NOAH

Yeah . . . and? You have been for about 20 years. You gonna finally get off your ass and do something about it?

KILLIAN

Yup. Just wanted you to know.

NOAH

Good. When you're done going all Romeo on her, can you put in a good word for me?

KILLIAN

We'll see if she even listens to me.

NOAH

Is she doing okay?

KILLIAN

How about you come here tomorrow and ask her yourself.

NOAH

She doesn't want me to do that.

KILLIAN

I think you might be surprised.

> She's been on the piano for hours.

NOAH

It's a start.

KILLIAN

> Yeah.

I shut my phone off and leave it on my nightstand.

I'm done waiting.

By the time I get to her piano room, the music has stopped, and she's jotting something down in another pink notebook. Always pink for my girl. But when she looks up, something cracks in my chest. "Jesus, you're beautiful, Lilah."

She blushes and closes her notebook. Her long blonde curls spill over her creamy, freckled shoulders, and a long red silk slip of a nightgown skims her body. The snow that started hours ago casts an ethereal glow, but it doesn't hold a candle to her smile.

"I finished the song," she whispers reverently.

"Oh yeah?" I cross the room in fast strides, needing to be closer. "What's it called?"

"Red Lips & White Lies." Her long lashes flutter when I stop in front of her. "I guess I was inspired by all the liars in my life."

Lilah

Chapter 19

**When the world gets too noisy, focus on your own voice.
It's the only one that matters.**

—Lilah's Secret Thoughts

"You still think I'm one of those liars, princess?"

I'm not sure how I'm supposed to think anything at all when Killian stands next to me in low-slung, black-jersey pajama bottoms and absolutely nothing else. Why are his bare feet so damn sexy? And my God, by the time I drag my eyes up to the ink covering his golden skin, stretched around a bicep that looks chiseled from stone, I start to wonder if I'm the one lying . . . Lying to myself. Because trying to convince myself I don't want him certainly feels wrong.

But then again . . . how much of us has always been a lie?

"Once upon a time, I would have believed anything you said . . ." I decide if we're going to have this fight, I need to do it on even ground and stand up. Not that it puts me even close to being on even footing with the stupidly sexy giant. "But that was before you proved you lie as much as everyone

171

else. The difference was how much I blindly trusted every word you said before you proved me wrong. I haven't made that mistake since then. At least, I didn't think I had. But I guess some lessons are harder to learn than others."

My heart hurts, remembering the heart-wrenching pain.

"You ready to do this, princess?" he growls and reaches for me but changes his mind and crosses his arms over his chest instead.

Thank God. I don't think I could handle this if he was touching me.

"I'll never be ready to do this *again*, St. James. But we might as well get it over with. Everything about you hurts. Having you here . . . in my space . . . every day . . . So willing to do whatever it takes to keep me safe, when I'm pretty damn sure you're a bigger threat than any stalker could ever be." My body vibrates with hurt and anger and lust and love. "Fuck you for making me feel this way again." I push at his chest, but he doesn't budge, just absorbs the blow. "I swore I never would." Another shove as the first tear falls, and I curse him again. "You broke me. After everything you said, to find *you* like that, with *her*." I lift my hand again, but this time, Killian catches my wrist. "How could you do that to me?"

He plants my hand against his heart, thrumming steady and strong. A beat I'll still feel in my sleep for weeks to come. "How could *I*?"

"Yes . . . How could you?" I try so damn hard to stay strong when I feel every inch of the pain like it was yesterday, not ten years ago.

Killian's shoulders tense, and he steps into my space without dropping my hand. "How could *you*, princess?"

The utter destruction in his voice stops me dead in my tracks, and my words get stuck in my throat. "What?"

"How. Could. You? You saw something that night and made a decision without ever talking to me. You didn't trust me enough to question what you thought you saw." He clenches his jaw so tightly, I'm shocked his teeth don't crack. "I had just told you, you were it for me. That I was never gonna love anyone else. And you thought you saw something and left. You didn't step in. You didn't fight for me. For us. You just assumed I was a piece of shit and walked away."

"Of course I did. I spent the first three years of high school watching you fuck around with every girl who wasn't me. That wasn't new. What was new was that you did it after everything you'd just said to me. How did you think I was going to react? I felt like I was in one of those air-hockey games on the boardwalk, getting bashed back and forth between both ends until you hit hard enough that I sunk into that stupid hole at the end of the table. One minute, we were friends. The next, you told me you loved me. And before the night was over, you were fucking Gia Petrillo. Did you think I wouldn't find out?"

"I didn't fuck her." His green eyes blaze with a fire stronger than the sun. "She drugged me."

"Bullshit—" The word is out of my mouth before I can truly register what he's said. "What?"

He pulls my hand away from his heart and moves around me until he's sitting on the piano bench, and I'm standing between his legs. Eye to eye. Then he takes both my hands in his. "I had two drinks and felt fucked up. Too fucked up. I was looking for you or Maverick. Then the night just got . . . foggy. I remembered feeling like I needed to sit down, or I was gonna fall down. Then nothing. The rest of the night is a blank."

"I'm sorry . . . *what*?" I stutter, trying to wrap my head around what he's saying but failing. "If the night's a blank, how do you know what happened?"

"Maverick. He helped fill in the pieces. He saw you leave in tears while he was hooking up with Gia's friend. When he went to go after you, she stopped him and said it was probably because you saw me with Gia. Said she'd been bragging that she was going to bag me before the party. Mav knew there was no way that would happen and decided to figure out what the fuck was going on."

The room spins around me, and I take a small step closer to him. "I'm so confused."

"When he found me, I was blacked out, not moving, and Gia was on top of me trying to get my boxers down."

"But your arms were around her. You were kissing her. Your pants were down." I try to block the image out, but it was burned into my retinas a decade ago. "Her black panties were in the snow next to a condom wrapper."

"Think about it, princess. Think about what that all looks like. But think about what was missing. Was I moving? Did you hear my voice? Did you see my face?" Pain and hurt and anger swirl together, straining against his voice.

And— Oh. My. God.

"Killian . . . Why—why didn't you say anything? I screamed at you. I sobbed and hit you when you came to see me. Why didn't you tell me?" My chest shakes with the force of my pained sob, like an injured animal begging to be put out of its pain. "I told you I hated you. Why did you let me?"

"Don't even go there, Lilah. You won't like the answer," he warns, but I don't heed the warning. I can't.

"Bullshit. You don't get to say that now. You can't tell me all this—lay it all at my feet after ten fucking years and then tell me not to go there. Who else knew? Who else knew she hurt you? Jesus Christ, I'm going to kill her."

Rage momentarily replaces hurt, and I see red.

"Easy, killer. By the end of the next day, Maverick, Jamie, and Noah knew . . . them and my parents." He sighs. "I had a fight coming up, and I didn't know what she'd given me. I needed to be tested."

"Holy shit. She drugged you . . ." I whisper as it starts to sink in. "Why didn't anyone tell me?"

"I tried to, and you wouldn't listen. It might not sound manly, but you hurt me too, Lilah. I spent the whole morning puking my brains out. Spent the afternoon in the hospital. Then went right to your house, and you didn't believe me. I tried to tell you, and you wouldn't listen."

I think back to that night . . . to the way his skin looked pale, but I thought that was because he was ashamed of himself, and suddenly, I'm the one feeling shame.

"Then, that next day . . . you came to Crucible and threw your necklace at me. You told me you never wanted to see me again." Killian lifts my chin, forcing me to look at him. "A few days later, you were gone, and you never looked back. I texted you after a few weeks, and you'd changed your number. I figured if it was that easy for you to believe I'd do that to you, we weren't as real as I thought we were."

He drops my face, links his arms around my waist, and pulls me closer. "But that's the part I'm sorry about. That's where immaturity came into play. I should have fought harder. I should have made you hear me. But I was a dumb kid, and it was such a fucked up situation. My mom wanted to press charges and lost her mind when I refused to. I didn't want the world to know what happened. That would still be hanging over my head if it had come out."

"Killian . . . Oh my God. You *should* hate me." I wipe at my tears but can't stop them. "I—I have no words. I—I . . . I don't even know what to say. I'm sorry doesn't feel like enough. You're right. I should have known. I couldn't understand how you could do that to me, but you never did. I'm the one who broke us."

He pulls me in again, closing the last few inches between us and presses his face to my chest. "Immaturity broke us, Lilah. We were young and stupid and didn't know how to

175

handle this massive thing that had been building between us for years. But broken doesn't mean destroyed. It doesn't mean it can't be fixed. You can still fight for broken things."

It's my turn to lift his face in my hands, and the weight of the moment isn't lost on me. "I was awful to you, Killian . . . for years."

His thumbs brush the tears from my cheeks. "We weren't ready yet. I think I always knew one day we would be. But we weren't ready before." He pulls me down onto his lap and presses his lips to my forehead. "This isn't on you. The guys wanted to tell you right away, but I wouldn't let them."

"Why not?" I ask with guilt eating me whole.

"Because I was pissed too. If I had listened to them and let them say something, maybe we could have avoided all this shit, but I didn't. This isn't all on you." He drags his lips down to my temple. "But what we do about it now . . . That's up to you."

My stomach tightens when he kisses away my tears.

"I've spent a lifetime loving you, Lilah. It was always going to be us. Even when you hated me, I loved you. Even when I thought I hated you, I loved you more." His hand skims up my neck and grips the back of my head, and my entire body tightens with the anticipation of his next words. "I figured out a long time ago that I'd never stop loving you. I just needed you to be ready to hear it. Remember what I said . . . When I kissed you, it was going to be *welcome home, I missed you*. I fucking missed you so much, princess."

"You remember?" I wrap my arms around his neck.

"Every fucking word."

My heart nearly bursts with so much wasted time and pain. "I've never loved anyone but you. I never stopped. I should have—"

Killian kisses me with all the emotion we've both been holding onto for all these years.

Love and hate and heartache warring with an unimaginable need and devastation.

His hands are everywhere. In my hair. On my arms. Dragging the straps of my nightgown down. Like a man possessed, he kisses me like I'm his oxygen. Like he needs me to breathe. Like I'm the only thing in the world that exists. Us. Here. Now.

"I'm sorry," I murmur. "I'm so sorry."

He bites my lip and tugs. "Shut up, princess. You love me, and that's all that matters . . ." He sucks my stinging lip between his, and I moan. "Say it again."

My smile is slow as it spreads against his lips, and I shimmy off his lap and reach out my hands. "I love you, Killian. I've loved you my entire life. Even when I hated you, I loved you." I take his hands in mine and tug. "Now take me to bed."

His sexy grin makes my thong wet and my body hot.

"No."

"What—?" I don't get to finish my thought before he picks me up and sits me on the piano, and a cacophony of keystrokes play a horrible chord beneath my ass while my question turns into a laugh. "You're crazy."

He drags his hands up my legs, under my nightgown, and tugs down my thong. "Crazy about you, princess. Now spread those legs and tell me your mine."

Lilah

Chapter 20

"*I*'ve only ever been yours, Killian. I brace myself on my elbows and plant a bare foot against his firm chest. Only ever yours."

Like a man on a mission and I'm the prize, he shreds my red lace thong and presses me back against the cool piano. "Do you have any idea how much I've missed you? I had you for one weekend, Lilah, then you shut down and pushed me away . . . again."

His rough hands run up my legs. "Never again, princess. No more pushing. It's you and me, and we're gonna fight, and we're gonna get pissed, but we'll work it out. No more shutting down. No more pushing away."

He runs his nose up my neck and inhales before scraping his teeth over that soft spot at the base, then soothing it with his tongue, and I gasp.

"I hate that nickname." I whisper the lie for old time's sake and smile.

"No, you don't. You never did."

Killian drags a hand up my leg, bunching the red silk nightgown as he goes. "Have you gotten yourself off since your birthday, Lilah?"

My breath falters, and this gorgeous man smiles.

Still the devil you know . . .

"Did you think of me fucking you while your fingers were filling your pussy, baby?"

Holy fuck.

"How am I supposed to think when you say something like that?"

"You're not." He grins as his gorgeous green eyes darken to nearly black.

My laugh dies in my throat when he slides a finger between my thighs and through my sex. "You feeling needy, princess?"

"Always needy for you." I drop back against the piano, already shaking when he slides one finger inside me, then another. My body pulses around him as want wars with need, both driving me higher. Needing more. Wanting it all.

I press my foot against him, backing him up. "I need you," I warn before I swing my legs down and slide off the piano and onto Killian's lap. "I need you inside me. On me. All over me. I need to feel you—"

I'm cut off when he wraps an arm around my waist and shoves his pajamas down with the other before he sits us back down. "Take what you need, baby. Just give me you. You're all I want. You're all I see."

I lift my hips and press Killian's cock against my sex as I brace my hands against his shoulders and slowly sink down, taking him inside me.

Pleasure tinged with pain spikes, as he stretches me so thoroughly, my body hums around him.

I move slowly . . . achingly slow, my eyes locked on his. Barely breathing. Wanting to make up for all the years we've missed. For all the hurt. For everything.

I bite down on the thick, corded muscle of his neck, holding back a scream when I finally take him completely in.

"Fuck, princess, take your time. I don't want to hurt you." His big hand cups my face and tugs me down to his.

Goosebumps pepper my skin as I wrap my arms around those broad shoulders I love and try to move. "God, Killian. I love you." I press my lips to his. "Only ever loved you."

"*More* . . . more," I pant between kisses, then lean my forehead against his when I can finally move. "I need more."

"Taking me like such a good girl, Lilah," he murmurs against my lips.

His praise is like a gentle, loving stroke against my oversensitive skin. And when he finally begins to move, I'm already so close.

His strokes are slow and lazy, like we have all the time in the world.

And then it dawns on me.

We finally do.

"Hey, Lilah . . ." He licks into my mouth and thrusts deep inside me. "Welcome home." He groans as his hips pick up speed. Grinding into me. Holding my hips against his. Creating the most delicious friction against my clit as his cock swells inside me.

Home . . .

I whimper as his words sink in, unable to form a coherent thought.

Lost somewhere between lust and love.

Chasing my orgasm.

Knowing he'll be here to catch me when I fall.

Killian sucks my neck while he fucks me furiously. He slides a hand between us, and the pads of his fingers play with my clit until I'm one giant nerve, exposed and at his mercy.

His other hand holds me so closely, carrying all my weight. In complete control, and for once in my life, I give over willingly.

It's overwhelming. Too much. Not enough.

It's everything.

"Don't stop," I beg and throw my head back.

"Fucking never, Lilah." He fucks me harder. Faster. Slamming up into me over and over and over again. So good that when my orgasm finally tears through me, thousands of stars splinter and shatter behind my eyes, and I come with his name on my lips, his love seared on my soul.

"So fucking pretty, princess," he rumbles in my ear, then holds my face, demanding my mouth. "And all fucking mine." His hips snap up, and I cry out, and any threads of the past I was clinging to pull and fray. "Tell me your mine, Lilah. Tell me your pussy . . ." The first thread snaps. "Your body . . ." Snap. "And your fucking soul belong to me, Lilah. You belong to me, and I belong to you. Only you. Fuck, princess . . . My whole life, it's been you."

And without thought or choice, every last thread snaps, and any tether to the past is gone. It's just him and me and right now.

I cry out as a second orgasm threatens to drown me and press my lips to his. "My whole life, I've been yours. In this life. In every lifetime. I'll only ever be yours."

Killian comes with a roar.

My name falling like a sacred benediction from his lips and reverence in his eyes.

*H*ours later, I lie in bed, my fingers tracing circles over Killian's chest, unable to close my eyes for fear that when I wake, it will all have been a dream.

"You were right, you know," I whisper into the night, feeling both strangely brave and yet completely vulnerable at the moment.

Killian buries his face in my hair and pulls me in closer. "You're going to have to be more specific. I'm right an awful lot."

I laugh quietly and keep tracing. "If you had kissed me that night at Crucible, I wouldn't have wanted to leave for my first tour. You're the only thing I've ever wanted more than music."

He rolls me over and looks down at me, love shining in his big green eyes. "We had things we both needed to prove to ourselves. You were already my world, Lilah. If we had taken things further, I don't know whether I'd ever have had the determination to do what I've done. I would have been fat, dumb, and happily lost in you for the rest of my life. At least when I do that, I'll be able to tell our kids I was a champion once."

"Our kids?" I squeak and trail my fingers over the strong angles of his face. "You think about our kids?"

He doesn't skip a beat. "Sure. I always thought they'd look like you, but now that I know from experience what dogs men are, I'm kinda hoping they're ugly. I don't know if I can take having daughters who look like you. Not unless we have sons first."

As if there were ever any doubt how long I've loved him, that one sentence just did me in in so many ways. "First, can we just ignore that you have experience being a dog with anyone but me, please? Because the thought of that makes me kind of stabby."

I pull his face down to mine and nip his lip. "But I can't wait to have your babies one day, Killian. I think the only thing I've ever wanted to be more than a singer is a mother."

"Is it too early to ask you to marry me, Lilah?"

My heart stops and starts all at once, and I smile against his lips. "Maybe a little."

"How about we start with you opening your birthday

present, then work our way up to a ring?" He teases. At least I think he's teasing until he gets out of bed and takes the unopened pink box from where it's been living on my vanity.

I sit up and wrap the sheet around myself as he sits back down and places the box in the palm of my hand. "Happy birthday, princess."

"Why am I nervous?" I ask with shaking hands as I untie the box and tear off the paper. A tiny red box sits in my hand, and my voice and my heart get stuck in my throat.

"Open it, Lilah," he tells me gently.

And my heart is no longer in my throat because it sinks to the floor.

I crack open the lid, and sitting neatly on a layer of red velvet is the golden strawberry necklace Killian gave me for my sixteenth birthday. "But how . . ."

"Princess." He wipes my eyes before I even realize I'm crying.

"But I threw this in the trash." And wished a million times I hadn't.

Killian shrugs and takes it out of the box. "Turn around."

I lift my hair and turn as he fastens it around my neck.

"I took it out of the trash and kept it. I guess I always knew I'd get the chance to give it to you again."

I climb into his lap and wrap myself around him like a spider monkey. "Thank you for keeping it safe for me."

"I will always keep you safe, princess."

Lilah

Chapter 21

You're the song I don't want to end.

—Lilah's Secret Thoughts

"Hey, Scottie." I answer the call and toss my phone to the counter. "You're on speaker, and my sister's here with me," I tell her and go back to the chicken I just pulled from the grill. Not gonna lie. I'm pretty proud of myself. This might be the closest I've ever come to cooking. Hopefully, it's not raw.

"Hi, Scottie." Dillan waves as if she's in the room and keeps scrolling through the contract she's reading.

"Okay well, let's get right into it then. I fired Tasha, reminded her of her NDA and had her severance sent to her. I wish I could say I was surprised, but very little surprises me anymore. Better people than her have been caught selling secrets. I just hate that they were yours. I guess it goes to show you everyone has a price." Scottie tsks like she's admonishing a child, and I want to scream.

"You're sure she was the leak?" I ask again, even though I know the answer. She'd been feeding information to the

Kroydon Kronicles and anyone else who wanted to pay for a story. Just the thought of it makes me physically ill.

"We're sure or we wouldn't have terminated her contract. Now listen, Iris needs to know if we're replacing Noah, and I need to know if we're looking for a new assistant."

Dillan looks up from the contract with wide eyes, suddenly very interested in the conversation. She knows the answer to one question but knows better than to ask about the other.

"Dillan is my new assistant. And before you say anything about working with family, she's already looking over her contract, and the decision is final. As for Noah . . ." I look away from Dillan and back down at the chicken. "I'm still not ready to make that call."

"Lilah—"

"I know, Scottie. But I'm not. And you can't tell me that if we need a fill-in at the last minute, we don't have ten guys in our arsenal completely capable," I snap, unwilling to discuss this. Not yet.

"I didn't say that, but I think you need to talk to Noah and make a decision. It's been weeks. If you wanted to forgive him, you would have already done it."

I grab the phone and walk through the kitchen door, fuming. "Don't you think I know I need to make a decision? This is my brother, not just my bassist, And I'll figure it out on my fucking time. I swear to God, I'd cut every last one of you completely out of my career if I could. So maybe think about that before you try to force me into a decision I'm not ready to make. You and Iris did the same damn thing Noah did, it just didn't hurt as badly because let's face it, to you and the label, I'm a dollar sign. But to Noah . . ." I trail off and spin around when the sliding glass door beeps as it opens behind me and Killian pops his head out.

"You okay, princess?" His voice wraps around me like a warm, weighted blanket, calming me.

I nod and press a kiss to his lips. "Yeah. I'll be in, in a second."

"K." He wraps an arm around my waist and drops a kiss on my head, and I wait until he's back inside before holding the phone back up.

"If you want answers, you need to give me answers. I want to know every single safety protocol that's being put in place for the remainder of the tour. Tell Iris if she wants me on that plane, she's got work to do first." I disconnect the call and look around the snowy backyard. It's beautiful and peaceful and everything I wanted when we planned this house, and I don't want to leave it. For the first time since I jumped headfirst into this career, it's more than just being tired. It's more than a lack of excitement over the wear and tear a tour causes.

I don't want to leave here.

I don't want to leave home.

And I don't want to leave Killian.

Ugh . . .

Back inside the kitchen, Maddox, Rome, and Killian stand around the counter, shoveling grilled chicken and brown rice into their mouths like it's their job to eat bland food, and in some way, I guess it is. The three huge men make this room feel small, and when I move in next to my sister, I can tell she's thinking the same thing.

"Everything okay?" I whisper, and Dillan smiles.

"Just thinking I'd like to be the cream between that Beneventi sandwich."

"Oh my God," I cackle, and every eye in the room turns my way.

Killian pulls me to his side, and Maddox groans. "You

guys plan on coming out to the family any time soon or are you gonna just keep doing a shitty job of hiding it?"

"The Kingston Foundation event is this weekend. Pretty sure the whole family is going to be there," Killian tells him as his fingers dig into my hip, and filthy thoughts flit through my head.

"Yup. Mine too, since half of them work for the Kings," I add. "Besides, I'm pretty sure the whole world heard about us at my birthday party. I think we were the intro for TMZ the next day."

"Yeah." Dillan pops a tomato in her mouth and looks between the brothers. "Well, maybe just try not dry humping each other on the dance floor this time. Grandpa is going to be there."

"Dry humping?" Rome laughs. "Oh—"

"Do not finish that sentence," I warn and pick up the knife from the counter. "And stay away from my sister."

Both brothers laugh this time as Killian holds my hand steady. "Uhh . . . maybe put the knife down, princess."

I shrug and put it back down. "I was just teasing."

"You're fucking nuts, Tinker Bell," Rome exclaims with a gigantic smile. "I'm here for it. You've been hiding a kinky vibe. If you ever get bored of that oaf, call me."

"Get the fuck out," Killian jokes, and Rome gives him the finger.

"Make me."

"Ohh . . . this sounds like fun," Dillan sighs, and I wonder exactly when my life went off the rails.

187

"Come on . . . I've been dying to go in the hot tub while it's snowing. Don't be a baby," I taunt Killian later that night, once we're alone. "And besides, it'll be good for your sore muscles."

His pupils are big and dark and taking over half his eyes as he stares at me in the red bikini I put on in hopes I'd get just this reaction. "Princess . . . it's cold out there."

"It is." I trail my finger down his bare chest, then drag my tongue along the same path. "But the hot tub will be hot, and I'll be even hotter."

I step back and turn away slowly, so he can get the full effect of the French cut, ruffled bottoms and the way they cup my ass, then dart out the door, knowing he's following.

"Fuck, woman." He watches me climb into the hot tub, then follows me in. "You're lucky I love you."

I sink under the bubbles and untie my bikini top, then fling it at his face and stay submerged so he can't see the goods. "I am very lucky you love me."

"Get that fine ass over here." Yum . . . I love when his voice does that growly thing.

"Uh-uh . . ." He reaches for me, and I think about backing away—but really, why the hell would I? "Killian . . ." I giggle and wrap my legs around his waist while I make sure to keep mostly submerged under water.

"Love that sound, Lilah."

I kiss the base of his neck, and his cock jumps under my ass. "Your name?"

"No, baby. Your laugh."

"Aww . . . you say the sweetest things." I lick up his neck and around his ear until he's squirming. "How was training today?"

In a move so smooth I don't even realize what he's doing until it's done, he unties both strings of my bikini bottoms and digs his fingers into my ass. "It was fine. How did everything go with Dillan? Did she take the job?"

He bobs up and down with me clinging to him so my boobs keep popping out of the water, covered in goosebumps. Apparently, men are simple creatures who are easy to please, at least according to mine. Feed him, fuck him, and show him my boobs. Not necessarily in that order.

"She did take the job. Scottie fired Tasha. And I basically threatened to fire Scottie, Iris, and Zoe. I think I need a sabbatical. I need to make a decision about Noah. I need to meet with Zoe soon to discuss PR strategy for the rest of the tour, and I'm sure I'm going to be lectured about this." I dig my fingers into Killian's hair and scrape my nails down his scalp until he's putty in my hands.

"Lectured about what?" He takes my hands away and kisses my wrists. "What did you do wrong?"

"Zoe has always been adamant that I not be overtly public with my dating life, and I kinda blew that to hell at my birthday party. Not to mention we've got the Kingston Foundation thing this weekend and then your fight coming up. She's not going to be happy." Killian traces my bottom lip with his calloused thumb, and I wonder if I could come just from that when I feel every second of the touch deep in my core.

"First of all, I'm not your dating life, Lilah. I'm yours, and I'm not going anywhere. So she's going to need to get over it. Second, if you want to get a new team, get a new team. You're the only Lilah Ryan. They need you. Not the other way around. Everyone except Noah. Him you're going to have to talk to at some point."

"I'm naked in your arms at night, in the snow, with my pussy rubbing against your cock, and you want to talk about my brother?" I tease and tug at his bathing suit.

"Nope," he answers as his mouth crashes against mine.

Lilah

Chapter 22

Your village doesn't have to be big. It has to be loyal.

—Lilah's Secret Thoughts

here's a knock at the front door a minute before it opens and Noah walks in, and I freeze. "What are you doing here?"

My words are barely audible over my crazy, thrumming heart.

"Guess I should have changed the gate code," I murmur and slide my other foot into my silver heel.

"Really?" Noah asks as he shuts the door behind him. "You look pretty, Tink."

I look down at the tiered, red gown that was flown in for me to wear to the Kingston Foundation benefit tonight. It's a beautiful piece of art, and I feel like the princess everyone likes to call me.

"Thank you. You look pretty snazzy yourself." Noah always rocks a tux like nobody's business. "And no. I didn't mean it when I said I should have changed the code. You just caught me off guard. I wasn't expecting you."

"Yeah well, I figured since you fired me, I wasn't exactly welcome." He shoves his hands into his navy-blue pockets and pouts. Yup, pouts. Because what else should a big brother do when you're mad at him. And I use the term *big* cautiously. Noah is six minutes older than me—and over a foot taller.

"Well, I assumed since you lied so well—"

"Jesus Christ," Killian groans as he walks down the staircase in his own tux and makes my brother look like a little boy playing dress-up. "You're both miserable without the other to talk to every day, and you know it. Kiss and make up. Life's too damn short." He drops a kiss on the top of my head. "You look beautiful, Lilah." He hands me his bow tie. "Can you tie this stupid thing for me?"

I look from him to Noah and feel like a complete asshole.

I take the tie from his hand and tuck it into his pocket. "Sorry, champ. I don't have a clue how to tie that. But it looks nice unbuttoned." I smooth my hands down his lapels.

"You okay?" he asks as he looks between my brother and me, and I nod.

"Yeah. Can you give me a minute?"

"Sure, princess." Then he runs his nose over my ear. "You look beautiful tonight. Any chance the panties match the dress?"

I giggle and press up onto my toes and whisper, "Who says I'm wearing panties?"

He groans, and I think Noah gags. *Shithead.* It's not like he heard what I just said. "Is this how it's going to be now? You two making out whenever you're together?"

"That's assuming you're around to see it," I snap, and Killian walks away, knowing I need to handle this myself.

Noah nods Killian's way. "Does that mean you two finally worked your shit out?"

"Yes," I answer softly because it's nobody's business but

ours. Actually . . . "You knew what really happened for years, and you never told me?"

There's no missing the hurt in my voice or the hurt on Noah's face at my words.

"It wasn't my story to tell, Tink. It was his. And he asked us not to say anything. You never asked me what happened, so I never lied to you, and Killer was dealing with his own shit. If that was how he needed to deal with it, we all had to respect that." It's pretty amazing how much you can love someone and hate what they did at the same time.

"I never knew you were so good at keeping secrets, big brother." The words come out more cruel than I intended, and guilt trickles in immediately.

Noah takes a step toward the door, and I reach out to stop him. "Don't— Don't go. I'm sorry. I shouldn't have said that. Believe it or not, I do know that you were trying to protect me. Misguided as you were. You can't protect someone with a lie, Noah. Especially when that lie actually put me more at risk."

He closes his eyes, and I see the tension he's keeping in his shoulders and the exhaustion lining his eyes that wasn't there before. "I swear to you, Tink, I thought I was protecting you. I trusted Scottie to know what was best, and I was wrong. I am sorry, and on my fucking life, I'll never do it again."

Scottie . . . Maybe it *is* time for a team shake-up.

My assistant was selling secrets to the paparazzi.

My publicist is constantly pissed about my choices.

My manager thinks it's safe to lie to me.

Which leads me to wonder what the hell else she's been lying about.

And there's still the issue of the stalker no one has heard from since the tour went on hiatus.

"Do you promise to never do it again?" I ask as I move

next to him and brush my hip against his, then lean my head against his shoulder.

"Yeah," he answers immediately and leans his head on top of mine. "Any chance you haven't replaced me yet? I hate the idea of you being out there for two months without me . . . Who's gonna make sure you survive on more than strawberries and ice cream?"

"There's a pretty good chance. I never told the label I fired you," I admit as Noah slides an arm around my shoulders.

"I'm sorry I fucked up."

I look up at my twin brother and know deep in my soul I don't want to tour without him.

"I think this is going to be our last tour for a few years. You okay with that?" I murmur, admitting it out loud for the first time.

"Yeah, Tink. That sounds good to me."

A minute later, Killian walks back in like the cat who ate the damn canary. "Okay, now that we're all good, can we please leave before my mother gives us shit for being late? You both know how she gets."

"Damn. I'm outta here. See you guys there." Noah kisses my cheek and waves at Killian.

"Chicken," I call out as the door clicks shut behind him. "You ready for this?" I ask Killian as I step into his arms.

"Ready for what? My family already knows about us. Rome has a big mouth. No way he kept it shut. And your family definitely knows because Dillan's crazy-ass mouth is even bigger than Rome's, and she might as well move in with us as much as she's here."

I giggle because nothing he said is wrong. "I mean, you're not wrong. But that's not what I was talking about. You think your life is high-profile. You're a world champion with a pedigree to back it up and a family legacy on both sides most people would die for a piece of. But trust me when I say none of that has prepared you for what stepping out with me will do to your life."

"Lilah Belle . . ." He circles my waist and drags me to him. "I've gone through the motions without you for years. There's not a damn thing you could do or say that's going to scare me away. Bring on the crazy."

"Are you sure?" I ask him, so scared he's going to change his mind. "I've never done this before, so the paparazzi is going to be rabid."

"Let them, baby."

Let them . . . I guess it's worth a try.

Killian

The top floor of the Four Seasons hotel has hosted the Kingston Foundation Awards for the past five years. The foundation recognizes achievement in humanitarianism in and around the city of Philadelphia, and this is one of the few events my entire family is expected to attend each year. Lilah's grandfather, Joe Sinclair, the former head coach of the Philadelphia Kings, is one of the recipients tonight, for years of quiet dedication to this city and the thousands of hours he's spent giving back. He could donate money—write a check and feel good about himself—but that's not his way. He knows he's getting the award tonight, but I don't think his family does.

And as the questions fly at Lilah and me from every direction when we walk along the gauntlet of press to get to the ballroom, I'm glad it wasn't announced ahead of time either. Or the whole world would know by now. Questions fly at us, left and right, and my girl smiles and holds my hand like a pro. She rarely answers except when a pushy older guy whistles, and she stops and looks at him. "Hey, Lilah. Any chance this is the guy?"

"What guy?" She smiles coyly, knowing exactly what she's doing.

"Your muse," he calls back. "You know . . . the guy."

Lilah looks up at me, absolutely fucking beaming, and I slide my hand from hers and wrap my arm around her waist. "His name is Killian St. James, in case you weren't sure. And he's not just the guy. He's always been *that* guy."

She leans up onto her toes and presses a kiss to my cheek, then keeps moving, and I do my best to just keep up with her.

Once we're inside the noisy ballroom, she relaxes for a moment. "You did well."

"You did all the talking, princess." I hold her closer. "Thanks for that, by the way."

"Anytime." She smiles. "Ohh, I see my sister and cousins."

"Go. I'll get us drinks." I watch her walk away, thinking about how badly I want to strip her out of that damn gown as I head for the bar.

"Stop thinking it, son." Dad comes up beside me and slaps my back. "Weigh-ins are tomorrow. Your fight is two days from now."

"You warning me about booze or sex?" I joke, knowing the answer is both, especially when the old man glares. I was already only getting a water for myself. But there's no way I'm not stripping that woman naked and sinking into her all night long later.

"I hear ya. You already know I'm two pounds under, and I'm gonna be fine for weigh-ins." I try to reassure him, but for as calm as Dad usually is, he's the opposite on fight weekends.

"I told your mother we should have rescheduled this event for a different date," he grumbles.

"What do you always say?" I argue, and the look he gives me says he knows exactly where I'm going here and isn't having it.

"You're a fucking beast, Killer. You're the fucking best. But even the best don't need distractions, and tonight is a distraction. That girl." He points to where Lilah is standing with her family. "She's a distraction."

"I'm going to marry that girl," I tell him, and fuck, if it doesn't sound even better out loud.

He claps my shoulder. "Just don't do it this weekend."

"Asshole," I grumble, and the old man laughs.

"One day you're gonna have your own kid, and they're going to drive you crazy, and I'm going to laugh my ass off. But right now, you're still my kid, and it's my job to make sure you're ready for this weekend."

"I'm ready." I force my eyes off Lilah. I'm ready for everything.

Lilah
♪♫

Chapter 23

Music makes my soul sing and my heart soar. What do you do?

—Lilah's Secret Thoughts

"*I* don't want you alone for even a minute tonight, Lilah. Promise me you'll either be with Jamie or Maverick or Maddox or Noah at all times. Keep your panic button on you, and let Xander hang as close as he wants to. The arena is going to be a fucking madhouse." Killian tucks my hair behind my ears. "And you find my team and stay with them from the minute we get there until you have to take your seat."

"Killian—I promise you, I'll do whatever you need me to do, so stop worrying about me and focus on you." I press up on my toes and kiss his jaw. "I love you. I'll be safe. Now go before you're late and your dad gets mad at me."

"I'm not worried about the fight, princess. That'll be the easiest part of the night. I'm worried about all the attention you're going to get that I won't be able to protect you from."

I bury my face in his hoodie and breathe in his clean,

crisp, oceany scent. "We should sneak away to a beach as soon as my tour is over. Just you and me and a hut over the ocean, where no one can see us and you can destroy every bikini I bring."

"With my teeth?" He grins, and I melt into a puddle of goo.

"Yeah, champ. With your teeth. Now go win me a fight, so I can plan this for us without your schedule getting in our way." I push him away and smack his ass. "I love you, St. James."

"So fucking much, Lilah Belle . . . So fucking much."

Killian

"*D*id you get it?" Maddox asks as Hudson tapes my hands, while the official stands there, watching and waiting to sign off on the move.

I nod but don't say anything. I'm gonna kill my cousin, and judging by the shit-eating grin on his pretty-boy face, the fucker knows it too.

"Get what?" Hudson asks as he switches to the other hand.

"Dude," Rome joins in, and I'm gonna fucking kill them all. "Did you get the ring?"

Hudson stops taping and stares at me. "Ho-ly fucking shit. Are you asking Lilah Ryan to marry you?"

"What the hell are you all gossiping like little fucking girls about over here?" Dad bitches, and Hud goes back to taping my right hand. Dad looks at each of us. "Nothing to say now? *Good*. Get your head in the fight."

Hudson rips the tape, then taps my knuckles and moves so the official can sign off on them. We're three fights out from mine. A solid twenty minutes, and the excess energy kicks in right about now, just like it does every time. Tonight, it's worse though. I walk over to Maddox when he pulls out his phone. "Is she out there?"

"Yeah, Mav's got her. You want her in here?"

"Yeah." For the first time in hours, the calm starts to settle, even with the look Dad is throwing my way.

A minute later, the doors open, and Maverick and Lilah walk in, and my head spins.

She's wearing a short purple-ish pink dress that ties around her neck and makes her tits look incredible. Her hair is pulled back at the sides and falling down her back in waves. Stacks of gold bracelets are around both wrists, and that old golden, strawberry pendant is around her neck. And when she sees me, her glossy pink lips split into the biggest smile as she practically runs into my arms. "Damn, baby. You look fucking hot."

"So do you, babe. You look kinda scary for everyone who isn't me," she teases, then looks around the room at all the people. "I don't think I realized your team is this big."

"It's fight night. Everyone is here. But Hudson, Dad, and Maddox are the only ones who will be on the cage." I look around the room and catch Hud's eye. "Hey. Can I have the room for a few minutes?"

He nods and fist-bumps me. "Focus, kid."

I nod and watch as he clears the room.

Dad doesn't look thrilled, but he leaves.

"Look at you, hot shot. You're all sorts of important," she teases, and this right here, this is what I needed. *Her.* She wraps her arms around my neck and digs her thumb into the muscle. "What's the first thing you want to eat after the fight?"

"You." I grin and lick my lips. "All night long."

"Killian . . ." she giggles, and that sound. Fuck me, that sound is everything.

"Fine. Tomorrow, I want blueberry pancakes from The Busy Bee. With a side of bacon and sausage, and real maple syrup, and a bigass glass of orange juice." I rest my gloved hands on her perfect ass and pull her closer. "But I swear to God, Lilah. You're all I want to eat tonight. I don't want to party. No bars. No clubs. I want to go home with you and celebrate." Truer words . . .

"Sounds like you better win then, champ."

I pull the ring from my pocket and hold it up in front of her. "Pretty sure that's up to you, princess."

"Killian," she gasps and steps back. "Oh my God."

Her smile is big and beautiful and tear-filled.

"Is that all you're going to say, princess?" I ask, smiling like a lunatic.

She rolls her lips together as she shakes. "You haven't asked me anything, champ."

"Marry me, Lilah Belle. We've wasted so much time already. I don't want to waste another minute. Marry me. Let me spend my life loving you and protecting you. I want to be your best friend and your biggest fan. I want my life to start and end with you in it. Every day. In every world. It was always going to be us. Marry me."

She nods and throws herself into my arms. "I would have said yes when I was sixteen."

"I should have just asked you then. It could have saved a shit-ton of heartache." I laugh as I capture her mouth in a searing kiss. "I love you, Lilah."

She holds her hand up and lets me slide the three-carat, brilliant-cut, pink diamond onto her finger, then brings her eyes back to mine. "It's stunning."

"I had a little help," I admit and enjoy the confusion

playing over her face. "I asked your mom and dad for permission, and your mom may have offered up an idea or two."

"You asked my parents." She sighs sweetly. "I bet that meant a ton to my dad, Killian."

"He warned me that you and your mom are nuts and to never say he didn't warn me."

There's a knock at the door before Maddox walks in. "It's time, man. Mav's waiting to take Lilah back to her seat."

She cups my face in her hands and smiles bright enough to light up the sky. "I love you, Killian St. James. Now go kick his ass so you can make good on that after-fight promise." She leans into me and kisses my ear. "I have on very special panties, just for you."

When she pulls away this time, she kisses me quickly, then drags her hand along my jaw, and I pull her back and kiss her ring. "You're gonna be my wife one day soon, Lilah."

"You bet your sweet ass I will. Now go win me a fight." And with that last word, she sashays out of the room, her hips swaying and ass teasing me in that short dress.

"She's fucking nuts," Maddox mutters, smiling.

"Yeah, she is. And she's gonna be my wife."

Lilah

Chapter 24

She's a queen, but she'll always have a tiny bit of crazy
hiding beneath the crown.
Test her at your own risk.

—Lilah's Secret Thoughts

"Chill, Tink," Maverick lectures as we take our seats, and I growl. Legit growl.

"Tell me to chill when it's the man you love about to be beaten up for five rounds," I snap, and Rome, who's already sitting down, curses me.

"First, bite your fucking tongue, Tink. He's not getting beaten up. He's gonna do the beating. And this fight isn't lasting all five rounds. I say he's got him before the end of the second. This is ending in a knockout, not in points."

"I don't even know what that means." Damn it. I should have paid more attention.

Rome shakes his head. "Title fights are five five-minute rounds. But your man doesn't ever take five minutes, does he?"

My face flushes, and I bite my tongue. No one needs to

hear about Killian lasting so much longer than twenty-five minutes.

I run my nervous hands over my dress, and Rome looks down and smirks.

"Damn . . . he did good."

I can't stop my smile, and my sister yanks my hand to her, nearly taking my whole arm with it. "Holy shit, Tink. Is that—"

"Damn," Noah kinda groans. "That son of a bitch finally did it."

Jamie pulls a twenty out, and so does Noah, and they both hand them to Maverick.

"What the hell?" I ask as the lights go down in the arena, and music starts pumping through the speakers. "Crazy Train" plays as the announcer introduces Victor "The Dominator" Domingo.

Maverick takes their money with a smile. "Don't be pissy, Tinker Bell. We made a bet in high school, and I just won. You two are engaged before you're twenty-eight. Jamie had thirty, and Noah had thirty-five."

"You fuckers bet on how old I'd be when I got engaged?" I ask, shocked and maybe a little annoyed. But maybe not.

"In all fairness, Tink. We bet on when you and Killer would get engaged. So we always knew it would be you two. The whole fucking world knew it would be the two of you." Jamie shrugs like he's imparting wisdom, and the lights in the arena flash as the song and the vibes of the entire arena change.

A single piano chord plays before Jay-Z's voice shouts out, followed by Rhianna's. Killian's entrance song is such a powerfully cool version of "Run This Town," spliced with "Posthumus Zone," and the entire arena jumps to its feet.

The lights flash purple in time to the beat as the announcer hypes the crowd.

Chills cover my body as I hear the deep voice announce, "And that's the sound of Killian 'The Killer' St. James making his way to the cage he called *his cage* yesterday at weigh-ins. The Killer knows this is his fight to make it or break it. Win, and he keeps his title. Win, and he becomes the most successful champion the legendary Crucible MMA gym has ever produced. The Dominator is here to win the title. The Killer wants to secure his legacy and step out of the shadows of his father and uncle. Which man is going to go home a winner?"

The crowd roars, and I grab Maverick's hand. "Oh God, I don't think I can watch this."

"I'm telling you, it's gonna be over fast, Tink," Rome promises, and I hold my breath.

Killian

"*A*nd for the final fight of the night, the heavyweight championship."

The ref drops his arm, and I tune everything out.

Hearing nothing but the buzzing white noise I've trained to drown out the rest.

My coaches' voices, the only ones I let in.

I see nothing but Victor.

Not the ref. Not my team or his.

Not my girl in the seats who I've entrusted to my friends.

Just my enemy and me.

"Let's go to war," Dad yells.

"With your shield," Hudson adds.

"Or on your shield," I growl back in response.

I step to the left, my body instinctively knowing Victor is going to attack out of the gate. He's scared and wants to get the first blow. But I've studied him longer, better, and closer. He goes right and misses me by a mile, getting nothing but air.

Anger is pushing him.

He's got something to prove, and it's going to make him faster to act. Slower to plan. Slower to think. Slower to observe. Nerves are ruling his actions.

He swings his leg out and misses. Again.

That's it, fuckface. Wear yourself out. Make this easier for me.

Even the best fighters—elite athletes—let nerves rule their fight.

Those fighters lose.

He has two more missed hits when I spin on fast feet with a jab, jab, jab.

I catch the corner of his jaw with an uppercut and grin when his head snaps hard to the side from the impact. Spit and sweat flying across the cage.

Yeah, baby . . . That never gets old.

He steps out to catch his balance and shakes it off, but I rang his bell, and he hasn't done shit yet. This sport is as much about mental toughness as it is physical.

And right now, he's shaken.

With his hands up, he stalks forward, not as energized now as he was sixty seconds ago but not giving up.

He's already slowing down, and better yet, he's making himself an easier target because his tell is showing. This guy is a great fighter. I've watched him in person. Flown halfway around the world to do it. Studied him. For fucking hours. He's good. Not great. Not me.

Pound for pound, he's strong and fights like it.

But this sport is more than strength.

But he's not me.

He hasn't trained like me. He hasn't lived this life his whole fucking life.

And it shows.

He's favoring his right leg.

Off-balance.

Fucking tells.

He's going to shoot out with his leg.

Not a chance.

"Take it to the mat," Maddox yells.

Already there, cousin.

I take him down so fucking hard, the cage rattles, and the crowd fucking roars.

My fists rain down hell over his face.

I shift my legs and lock them around his hips, immobilizing him.

He's fucked. Locked in place because he needs his arms to protect himself.

He can't fight when he's too busy defending.

I bring my elbow down as he turns his head and strike his cheek.

The crack of bone on bone is deafening.

His eyes roll back but stay open. Fuck, that's gonna hurt.

I take advantage of his daze and do it again.

This time my elbow connects with his nose.

Blood sprays from his nose, soaking the mat, but I don't stop.

Sorry, man.

I do it again, and he chokes back the blood now flowing into his mouth, so the ref doesn't call the fight, and shifts, trying to break my hold on his hips.

Not a chance, motherfucker.

"Stop playing and end this, Killer," Hudson shouts.

He's louder than Dad. Always louder during fights.

Victor shifts his hips, lifting us both off the ground, and breaks my hold on his legs.

Fuck.

I lock my arm around his neck, and he flips us over and slams me back into the mat as the buzzer sounds, and round one ends.

Shit. Not how I wanted this round to go.

My eyes immediately snap to Lilah's, inherently knowing where she is. And once I see her and know she's safe, I move to Dad, Hudson, and Maddox, who all yell at once.

"Focus."

"Breathe."

"What the fuck are you thinking?"

Their words mash together as I swish water around my mouth and spit.

"You good?" Dad asks, and I nod and look at Lilah one more time. She's surrounded by the men I trust most in this world. She's safe, and she's mine. I'm good.

"Yeah," I nod, breathing heavy.

"Then fucking finish him," Dad snarls, his calm breaking. "Don't let this go to round three, you hear me? You're the better fighter. Make sure he knows better than to ever challenge you again."

I nod and shake out my arms.

Round two starts, and Victor rushes me, managing to pin me against the cage.

But his grip is sweaty and sloppy.

He's already breathing hard before my fists fly against his ribs, over and over until I can force my foot out and leverage it to flip us around.

I press his face against the cage and slide my arm around his neck. "Tap, motherfucker," I grunt as I cut off his oxygen.

His face turns purple as he fights to get free.

"Choke him out," Maddox yells.

He tries to shift. To get under my grip. To kick. Desperation showing as he tries to free himself.

Until finally his fighting slows and eventually stops, and I drop him to the floor.

It's like I'm in an airlocked tunnel for a second with no sound escaping before the arena explodes. The ref moves between us as the medics rush in, but as soon as I released my hold, Victor started coming to.

"The three-time world heavyweight champion, Killian St. James."

Dad and Hudson rush the cage, but I tune them both out as I catch my cousin grabbing my girl. With Maddox pulling her forward and Rome shielding her from behind, they help her into the cage, and she runs for me. "You did it, champ!" she screams.

Blood and sweat cover me as she throws herself into my arms, and I lift her from the mat and squeeze her to me. I kiss her like we're alone and there aren't a hundred thousand people streaming this fight. "I fucking love you, Lilah."

She pushes my sweat-soaked hair from my face and kisses my brow, my cheek, my lips. "I love you so much." She holds my face still in her hands and kisses me over and over as she ignores everyone around us. "Holy shit, that was so hot. I'm so proud of you."

"Yeah, baby. That was just the start," I warn her, knowing when we get home, the celebration really begins.

The announcer moves next to us and shoves a microphone in my face. "That was an incredible fight, Killer. Is there anything you'd like to say?"

I set Lilah on her feet but anchor my arm around her waist, refusing to lose her in the crowd. "I'd like to thank my entire team for spending a lifetime training me and training *with* me. Crucible MMA is the best gym in the world with world-class coaches, and I'm fucking lucky they're my family. Victor put up a good fight tonight. One day, he'll have a belt. But not this one. This is my town. My belt." I squeeze Lilah extra tight. "And I fight for what's mine."

"Are you gonna take some time off now, or are you eyeing your next fight already?"

I blow out a breath and press my face into Lilah's hair. "I'm gonna take some time off. Maybe enjoy a honeymoon and figure out what's next."

"Are you thinking about retiring?" the ass asks, like he's gonna get an answer to that.

"I think I'm going to spend a few months as a groupie and figure things out from there."

Lilah laughs and turns her face away from the cameras.

Her hand lays flat against my chest, and her ring shines bright enough to blind the camera guy.

My town. My belt. My wife.

Lilah
♪♫

Chapter 25

Dance in the center of the storm.
Let the music soothe your soul and heal your heart.
Not a bad lyric.

—*Lilah's Secret Thoughts*

"*I* thought you said it was just us tonight." Killian buries his head in my neck and pulls me against him once he sees the friends and family filling my house a few hours after the fight.

"Oopsie," I whisper. "Everyone wanted to celebrate, and I couldn't tell them no. Between Dillan and Rome, food was ordered, booze was ordered, and Xander was basically losing his mind over the security aspect of it all."

"Lilah," he grumbles so only I can hear him. "You and me and blueberry pancakes. That's all I wanted. You—naked—with nothing but that ring on your finger."

"And you'll have it. I promise. Just as soon as they all leave." I frame his face with my hands. "I love you. You know that, right?"

"Yeah, princess. I know."

"Good. Because here comes your mom, and she's pissed." Basically announcing to the world we were engaged before we announced it to our families didn't exactly sit right with Scarlet St. James. No shocker there. This woman runs a billion-dollar empire. She's not big on surprises.

She stops next to us and hands me a glass of champagne, then taps her crystal flute against mine. "To the real prize."

My eyes grow wide as I look from Killian to his mother, confused.

Scarlet shakes her head. "We all knew it would be the two of you eventually." She lifts my hand and smiles at her son. "You did well, Kill." She kisses his cheek, then purses her lips. "Now give us a minute."

He doesn't move until I smile. "Go. I'll find you."

And moving a little slower than usual, the man I love more than anything in the world walks away, sore and tired and not at all in the mood to deal with a house full of people. I make a mental note to surprise him with blueberry pancakes from The Busy Bee in the morning.

Scarlet links her arm through mine. "Walk with me, Lilah."

You'd think it was her house, with the way she walks me out of the crowded family room and into my quiet music room. She drags a finger along the piano, and my cheeks flush, thinking about exactly what her son has done to me on the instrument. If Scarlet notices, she's gracious enough to ignore the reaction. "How are you doing? Watching them fight can be hard."

"I'm fine. Just glad it's over. I think he's a little frustrated by all the people here though." I'm not sure what she wants to know, but I don't think that was the real question.

That's still coming.

"It doesn't get easier, you know," she muses as she walks over to the wall of windows and looks out at the stars.

"Watching the people you love subject themselves to the same pain over and over again. It takes a toll on us as much emotionally as it does on them physically."

Now we're getting somewhere.

She's not talking about tonight's fight.

"I guess it's good that we learn from each fight then. It gives us a chance to understand what happened, so we don't make those same mistakes again," I counter, and a predatory grin spreads on Scarlet's face. "He never told me what happened in high school," I admit, showing my hand, unwilling to play this game of words with Killian's mother.

"But you know now."

"I do. And we worked it out between us, which is exactly where it's going to stay," I warn, because I'm not sure where she's going, but if she's about to try to warn me off her son or tell me I'm not good for him, she's about to have a hell of a fight on her hands.

She blows out a breath, appearing almost regal.

Like a queen readying for battle.

"He may be the fighter, but you're the stronger of the two of you. I'm going to need you to remember that. You will be his home. His anchor. You'll be his why. That's a heavy crown to wear. But you were born to wear it, Lilah. Your mother and I had many nights with many drinks over the years, and we knew it back then too. Don't give up on your love, and don't let him either." She runs her hand over the cool window, then turns to look at me. "I hate what you both went through in high school, but you both needed to see what was out there in the world to know you were what each other needed."

"I hate that I couldn't see what was right in front of my face," I admit, disappointed in myself. "I wish I could go back and stop it from happening. I hate that she got away with it.

212

She should have hurt the way we did. She should have hurt worse."

"Oh, sweet girl." Scarlet wraps an arm around me and lowers her voice. "She didn't get away with anything. Like I said, you're the stronger of the two of you. And so am I. We women generally are. And no one will ever hurt my family and get away with it. That goes for you too. You're part of the family now. And we're more powerful than most people could ever fathom. If you need anything at all, you ask. Do you understand?"

"No," I whisper, shocked by her confession that's also a non-confession.

Scarlet skips over any mention of Gia Petrillo. "You know King Corp. is always looking for good investments, and I heard you may be shopping for a new label."

"What— How . . . ?" I swallow and fight to keep my breathing steady. "Huh?"

"I've always loved music. We should talk before you leave on your tour. Stop by my office Monday. Bring Noah if you want, but leave your manager at home. This is between family. If you want to involve her later, go ahead."

"I don't understand," I whisper, not comprehending what she's trying to tell me.

"Lilah, I'm going to give you the opportunity to own your music and your label and your future. A partnership. If you're going to be a member of my family, no one should ever have the right to dictate your life to you ever again. You've earned that, Kingston or not. I've followed you. I know your numbers. I know your worth. I want to make sure you know it too." She tugs me along as she starts to walk. "Come to the offices Monday. My morning is open."

We walk, arm in arm, out of the music room and follow the sounds of celebration back to the others. "Oh—and Lilah . . ."

I stop and look at my future mother-in-law, a little shaken.

"Don't even think about eloping. I have one son, and I want to dance with him at his wedding. You'll understand one day." She leans in slowly and kisses my forehead. "Welcome to the family."

Holy. Shit.

J pick up the last of the glasses and add them to the dishwasher as Killian yanks the garbage bag from the cabinet, sulking.

"It's not that late," I giggle, and he drops the bag and storms across the room like I just rang the bell at the start of the fight. He lifts me up and plants my ass on the counter, then steps between my thighs.

"I asked you to marry me six fucking hours ago, princess. I was supposed to be buried inside you four fucking hours ago. Only I've had to play nice with my parents and yours. Our friends. Our cousins. Fuck. Half of Kroydon Hills was in your house tonight, cockblocking me." He looks pitiful as he pouts and is still somehow the sexiest man I've ever seen.

"Our house," I correct him, then wince. "I mean, I'd like it to be our house. I love this house and hoped when I built it, I could make it feel like home. I didn't know that what it needed to feel that way was you. But it did. You make it home, so I'm kinda hoping since you're stuck with me forever, maybe you'd agree to live here . . . with me?"

I drag the tip of my finger gently over the bruise blooming on his jaw, then run my lips along the same trail.

"So long as you're with me, I don't care where we live,

Lilah. Where you are, I'll be. Whether that's here or on a tour bus. No more distance. We've done that. It's you and me now."

"Killian," I sigh as he leans in and licks up my neck. "You can't go on tour with me. You've got a life and a job and training. It's two months, and I can fly home between a few of the stops."

I whimper when his teeth scrape my rapidly racing pulse point.

"Want to try that again? Because you can bet your perfect little heart-shaped ass you're not going on this tour alone." Killian plants a palm flat against the counter and dares me to challenge him as his other hand slides up the leggings I changed into once we got home.

God, I love this man.

"No snappy comeback, baby?"

I shake my head and run my hands under his t-shirt.

"Just thinking about how fucking hot I've been for you all night tonight, champ." I lean in and nip his ear. "How wet and hot—"

No sooner do the words leave my mouth than my leggings are ripped from my legs and his sweatpants are shoved below his ass. "Not gonna be gentle this time, baby. That okay?"

"I don't want gentle." I crash my mouth to his and bite down on his lip, nearly drawing blood when he slams his cock inside me in one powerful move.

He lifts me from the counter, and I link my legs around his waist and my arms around his shoulder as he holds me like a rag doll while he pounds into me over and over and over again. Hitting that spot that blows my mind every time.

"Fuck, princess. I'm not gonna last this time."

"Oh God, Killian. I'm so close." The whole night has been

one giant tease. Like foreplay on crack. And the stroke of his cock brings me closer to that high that's just out of reach.

"Fuck yeah, you are. Having you there." He drags himself out and digs his fingers into my bare ass. "Having you watch me."

I hang on for dear life when he thrusts back up.

"Knowing you were my prize. That this tight little cunt was mine, and my prize was going to be losing myself inside you all night. Fuck, baby. Nothing in the world better than that."

Oh. My. God.

Killian roars his release, and that's it.

That's all it takes for me to shatter around him.

He slows his thrusts, working me through my orgasm.

I gasp for air and press my lips against his. "I think we're going to need our own plane and maybe our own floor of the hotels, so we can do that whenever we want without anyone hearing us."

"Let them hear, Lilah. We've got ten years to make up for."

"Let them hear, huh? That sounds like a good song title to me," I joke as he sets my feet on the floor and kicks off his pants.

"You gonna write a song about me, princess?'

"They've all been about you, champ." I pull my t-shirt over my head and stand naked in front of him, loving the way I look in his eyes. "Every single one."

Lilah

Chapter 26

**You look happier – Thanks, five orgasms in seven hours.
It's good for the soul.**

—Lilah's Secret Thoughts

I slip out of bed the next morning and jump in the shower, *alone* and deliciously sore.

Who knew Killian would have that much energy after a fight? I figured he'd have been exhausted.

Well . . . I was wrong.

Once I've scrubbed and buffed every inch of my body and shampooed and conditioned my hair, I get out, dry off, blow dry, and throw on jeans and Killian's Crucible hoodie. Time to get my man blueberry pancakes with a side of so much pork, I'm less sure that isn't the main course with a side of pancakes. But it's what he wants, so I'm going to get it for him.

And because I'm feeling a little extra feisty this morning, I shove my panic button in the pocket of my jeans, kiss Killian's forehead, and sneak out alone for the first time in weeks. It shouldn't feel this good, but damn, it feels amazing.

March is always one of those weird months in Kroydon Hills. You never know if you're getting snow or rain. No surprise this year, there's still snow on the ground. It's turning to dirty mush, but it's still there. I smile as I slide behind the wheel of the Rover and head into town with the heat blasting and the sunroof open, just to get a little extra fresh air.

I don't know if it's the freedom of being out and alone, or the freedom I feel from knowing I'm loved and in love that's doing it, but I can't hold in my smile as I drive, singing at the top of my lungs to an old Journey song my mom used to love.

No one bothers me when I walk into the café across the street from my aunt's dance studio and my other aunts' lingerie shop. I place my order and wait at the counter, staring at Main Street. Half the street is made up of shops owned by my family or Killian's, and it's got me thinking about Scarlet's offer. I never considered buying into a label. I've only recently started seriously considering leaving Controlled Chaos, but I never thought about creating something from the ground up. And now that I have, I can't stop.

Noah and I used to talk about starting our own label when we were kids.

I told him I wanted to name it Blue Bell Records, after the street we grew up on.

Maybe it's not too late . . .

"Lilah Belle, what are you doing here?" Uncle Cooper pulls out the chair next to me and smiles when the waitress fills his coffee cup and hands me my bag.

"Just thinking about what-ifs . . . That and picking up blueberry pancakes." I hop off the chair and kiss his cheek. "I'm heading home now."

Uncle Cooper looks around. "Are you alone?"

I look down and smile. "Please don't yell at me. I just

came right here, and now I'm leaving to go right home, I swear."

"Hey, Dolly," Uncle Coop calls out to the waitress. "I'll be right back." He takes the bag from my hand and walks in front of me. "Come on. Let me walk you to your car."

Once we're outside, he looks around the sidewalk like he's expecting an ambush.

I guess some habits are harder to break than others. "Lilah, you can't do this right now. You can't sneak out. There's a reason you have security, and by sneaking out, you're not only putting yourself at risk, but you're putting the people around you at risk too. Not to mention, can you even imagine what it would do to the people who love you if something happened? You can avoid it all by taking this seriously and following the rules."

Knowing it and hearing it from your former Navy SEAL uncle are two slightly different things, and the guilt immediately churns in my stomach. "I'm sorry," I murmur, and he presses his hand to my back and walks me to my car.

Uncle Coop opens my car door and checks inside before he lets me behind the wheel. "I love you, kid. Make smart choices."

"Are we still talking about my security or did we veer off somewhere into an after-school special about the dangers of sex and drugs?" I can't help the sass that flows freely. He made it too easy.

He shakes his head and holds onto my door. "Both, you little smart ass. Damn. You are so much your mother's daughter, it scares me sometimes." He kisses the top of my head and leans back. "I hear you're even marrying your brother's best friend."

I hold back my quiet laughter. "Just like Mom did. I hadn't thought about that."

"I'm happy for you. I've known Killian almost as long as

I've known you. He's a good man. Now get home before he can freak out when he realizes you're not there. Drive careful." Uncle Coop shuts my door and taps my hood, then steps back and watches while I pull away.

I hate that he's right and that what I just did was stupid.

There goes my happy little bubble from this morning.

*W*hen I pull up to my gate, Zoe is there, talking to Xander, and I know I'm screwed.

Oh well. I'm not in the mood to be lectured by either of them.

Scarlet's words filter in again.

Maybe it is time to replace my team.

I pull through and wave at them both.

"Lilah," Xander starts the second I get out of my car.

"Don't," I stop him. "I'm sorry. I shouldn't have gone without you or Killian. I just—" I shift uncomfortably, guilt eating at me. "I just wanted to be normal for a minute. I wanted to do something for him for a change."

"I can't do my job, if you don't let me, Lilah," Xander tells me with a level of anger in his voice I'm not familiar with.

"I'm sorry. It won't happen again," I promise and turn to Zoe. "Did we have a meeting I forgot about?" I go through my calendar in my mind but know I'd never have agreed to meet the morning after Killian's fight, and I wouldn't have said let's meet at my house.

"No. But Scottie and I were talking about all the things we still have to discuss before the tour kicks back off, and that was before you announced your engagement to the world last night *before you told either of us.*" The chastising tone sets my nerves on edge.

I've had enough.

I push my door open and hold it for her. "Well, you're here now, so you might as well come in."

Her eyes zero in on the ring on my finger, and what looks like a flash of anger appears before it's gone just as quickly. She steps aside and waits for me to walk in before she follows me to the kitchen.

I pull the tins of food out of the to-go bag and set them in my warming drawer, then plant my hands on my hips and try to decide how to handle her just showing up at my house out of the blue.

I seriously need an extended sabbatical.

At least a year of writing without worrying about touring or recording.

Just living.

"Okay." I pull myself up to sit on the counter and smile, thinking about what we did right here last night. "Might as well get this over with. How bad are they spinning my engagement? Do they think I'm pregnant? Spinning out? Addicted to drugs and covering up rehab?"

All things, might I add, I've been accused of before.

She places her Birkin bag on the chair next to her and rummages around inside for something, then pulls out a tablet. "Well, let's see. I think the most pressing is that Killian made it appear that he was going on tour with you when you leave. We can't have your fans thinking that. Little girls look up to you. Killian is what their mother's warn them against. A bad boy who beats people with his hands. He can't come on tour with you, Lilah. I really wish you'd consulted me before you—"

"What?" I snap, pissed.

Truly angry. Not just annoyed.

Not just tired of being told how to live my life.

"You think I should have asked you before I wore my engagement ring?" I hop right back down from the counter, any pleasantries I was going for now gone. "I am so tired of this shit. I'm happy for the first time in forever. Can't you just be happy for me?"

"It's not my job to be happy for you. It's my job to protect you from the vultures. It's my job to keep them at bay." She takes a step closer. "It's my job to make sure you are taken care of, and since he's come into the picture, you've made that very hard for me."

"What?" My head spins. "It's not your job to make sure I'm taken care of. Why does everyone want to claim owner-ship of that aspect of my life? Why don't you all understand I can take care of myself?"

"Because you can't," she tells me calmly as she takes another step closer, and I suddenly feel uncomfortable. "Because I've always taken care of you, Lilah. I took care of you when you were young and naive and never stopped. You've always let me take care of you."

"I'm sorry—" I sound like a broken record. I'm so confused. "What?"

"Where is Killian? I think he should be down here for this." She looks around, like Killian will appear out of thin air.

It's wrong. I'm not sure what it is, but everything about her . . . and about this entire interaction is wrong.

That's the only excuse I have for what I do next.

"He left earlier." I cross my arms over my chest to hide my nervous fidgeting. "He's at the gym, debriefing with his team. He won't be back for a few hours."

"Fine." Zoe cracks her neck from one side to the other and pulls her hand out of the pocket of her coat. Then, my entire world shifts and threatens to shatter.

"Zoe . . . What are you doing with a gun?"

"Step away from the counter, Lilah." She points toward her purse. "There are zip ties in my purse. Could you get them for me please?"

"What the fuck?" I stand, shocked in place. "Zoe—"

"Lilah, please, my love. Don't make this hard. I know things have been difficult lately, and the fighter has made things worse. But once you're away from him, we can be together. Don't you see that?"

"You're insane," I hiss, wishing I'd gone back to Uncle Cooper's self-defense class. I look around the room for a weapon, not wanting to scream and wake Killian. I don't know what she'd do if she saw him. Would she shoot him? My God. Would she kill him?

Zoe trains the gun on my face, and I flinch. "I'm sorry. I'm so sorry," I cry. "I didn't mean it. You just . . . you scared me, Zoe. You've got a gun. Why—why do you have a gun?"

"I have a gun because I needed to get your attention, and I didn't know if I'd need it to get rid of the fighter. But now that it's just us, I don't need it, do I, Lilah? You're going to come with me because you love me the same way I love you."

"I—" Holy shit. What do I say? "I'll—"

I hear the first creek of the stairs and cringe, hoping she doesn't hear it too.

"I'll go with you. Let's go. If we go through the back door, Xander won't notice I'm gone. It'll be easier. Let's go." I go against any survival instinct I may have and move closer to her. "Please, Zoe." Tears stream unchecked down my cheeks when Killian's voice calls out for me.

"Princess . . . you down here? I thought we could go out for pancakes."

Zoe's eyes harden on me. "You said he wasn't here. You *lied* to me."

"Let's go. Right now, Zoe," I sob. "You and me. Nobody has to get hurt."

I try to walk by her. Try to get her to look at me instead of the doorway Killian should be crossing through any minute, depending on what room he searches in first. But she doesn't let me. Her dark eyes look wild when she takes the butt of the gun and smacks me across the face.

Pain rockets through my skull like I've never felt before, and the room spins around me while I fight to stay on my feet.

"Lying isn't good for your image, Lilah."

Oh, God. She presses the gun to my chest, and I hold back my scream.

Please don't let him come in here and see this.

But he's going to come in, and then what?

I think about my phone in my pocket, then remember that I shoved my panic button in there too.

Will she notice if I move my hand?

Do I take the chance?

Do I have a choice?

I reach for her with one hand, hoping like hell it throws her off and reach into my jeans with the other. My finger manages to press my panic button before she swings me off her. "I loved you, Lilah."

"Loved?" Killian asks as he walks into the kitchen, completely clueless as to what's going on.

I take the split-second of confusion to dart in front of Zoe as she swings the gun on Killian and fires.

Killian

Chapter 27

"*N*o—" I yell as Lilah falls into my arms, and the woman on the other side of the kitchen screams.

"You!" she shrieks and raises her gun. "You did this. That should have been you."

She aims the gun at Lilah, and I cover her with my body.

Everything happens all at once.

Glass shatters around us, and the woman with the gun falls to the floor as pain rips through my shoulder. Xander rushes in, barking orders into a phone and drops to his knees next to me.

"She shot her. She needs an ambulance." My voice is hoarse, and my ears won't stop ringing. "Lilah." I lift her in my arms and cradle her head. Begging. "Baby, please open your eyes. Lilah . . . *LILAH*—" I scream when she doesn't move and refuse to let her go when Xander tries to take her from me. "Get a fucking ambulance."

Her lashes flutter, but her eyes don't open.

"Lilah . . . baby. Open your eyes. You're going to be okay. Please, baby. Please." I press my lips to hers, then pull back and see a trickle of blood slip past her lips. "Lilah . . ."

I have no idea how much time goes by before the paramedics rush in and try to force me away from her.

"Killian, you've got to let them take her," Xander tells me, but I refuse to.

"I'm going with her," I tell anyone who comes near her until Xander pulls me away from Lilah.

"You've got to let them help her. I'll get you there right behind her. But you gotta let them help her first." He has to physically hold me back as the two men and one woman in uniform go to work, and a cop walks toward me.

"Can you tell me what just happened?" the officer in blue asks.

"I don't have a fucking clue." I refuse to take my eyes off Lilah, and when I swear I hear my name on her lips, I shove my way through everyone to get to her. I take her hand in mine and wince. Her hand is fucking freezing. "She's freezing," I yell at whoever the hell will listen.

"It's the blood loss." A different officer moves next to me. "Has anyone checked you out yet, son?"

They cut my hoodie off her body and have a pile of white gauze, which is now bright fucking red, pressed against her abdomen.

"I'm fine." I try to ignore him and move with the medics as they get ready to take her from me. "Just fix her."

I refuse to let go.

"Son, you've got to let them go." He looks around, blocking me. "Do we have anyone who can take a look at him?"

"I'm not staying here." I shove my way past him and grab Xander, staring at my hands that are soaked with Lilah's blood, gripping Xander's gray shirt. Fuck. "I need to get to the hospital."

He turns to the cops and tells them something, but I don't hear it.

I don't hear anything over the roaring in my ears.

Once we're in the car, the world starts coming back into focus.

"What—what the fuck just happened?" I ask, unsure if I'm asking Xander or myself. "Was that the publicist?"

"Zoe," Xander agrees and hits CarPlay. "Call Noah Ryan."

The phone rings before Noah answers, and I don't give Xander a chance to talk. "Get to the hospital, Noah. It's bad, man. I tried to stop it, but I was too late."

I run my hands over my face and look at them again.

They're wet.

I'm wet.

Fuck. I'm crying. I didn't even realize I was crying.

Noah asks a million questions all at once, none of them registering with me.

"Call your parents. Tell them the publicist shot Lilah. Tell them I'm sorry. I tried to stop it, but I was too late. They're taking her to the hospital now—"

"What hospital?" he screams, and the sound is something, like you'd hear from a broken fucking animal, being ripped from his throat.

Shit. I didn't even think to ask.

"They're taking her to UPenn. They have a better trauma center than Kroydon Hills," Xander tells him. "Call your parents, Noah. Then call Killian's. I'll call if we hear anything before you get there."

"Where's Zoe?" Noah asks, his voice at an unnatural decibel.

"Dead," Xander answers, and I turn to look at him.

"How?" I'm not sure if I'm asking how it happened or how I missed it.

"I killed her."

"*P*lease let a doctor look at your shoulder," my mother pleads for the millionth time in the past four hours, like I'm going to give her a different answer now than I did then.

"I'm fine. It's a graze. Brynlee looked at it, Mom." I look down at her from the place on the wall I claimed after the last time the nurse came out and updated us.

"Brynlee is a physical therapist, Killian. You might need stitches."

"Give him some space, Mom," Brynn saves me. "He's okay." She slides in next to me, taking up her own space on the wall, and waits for Mom to sit back down with Dad. "She's just worried about you, and you know she can't stand it when she can't control everything in her world. It's her love language."

"Yeah . . ." I look down at my blood-stained shirt that I refuse to change and squeeze the hoodie they cut off Lilah earlier between my hands.

"She's going to be okay, Killian."

She's going for comfort, but it misses its mark. "You can't know that, Brynn." I breathe in and out, trying to control—*fuck*—trying to control anything I can. Clinging to the idea that this is all a bad fucking dream. That we're going to wake up, and she's going to be sleepy and soft in my arms where she's supposed to be.

"I can . . . Big sisters know these kinds of things." Brynn leans her head on my shoulder and sighs. "Does she make you happy, little brother?"

"I know what you're doing," I tell her.

"Do you?" she asks quietly. "Do you remember my answer when you asked me that?"

I think back to that day in Brynn's condo when I found out she was seeing her now-husband and how pissed I was. "You said he was everything."

She nods slowly. "And *you* told *me* he wasn't everything, I was. Well guess what?" She waits me out then nudges me. "No guesses?"

"Brynn . . . I'm covered in the love of my life's blood. I'm not in the mood for guessing games," I grunt.

"Here's the thing, Killer. You were wrong. We both were. Because when you love someone the way I love Deacon and you love Lilah, one of you isn't everything. It's the two of you together that are everything. And there's no way you'd be given that for it to be taken away so quickly. I have faith."

"Wish I did," I utter, still wishing it was just a dream.

"Well, I believe enough for the both of us."

"Mr. and Mrs. Ryan?" When I look up, it's not the nurse calling us to her this time, it's a doctor. And I don't give a shit that I'm not Mr. and Mrs. Ryan when I approach. The doctor looks from Lilah's parents to me, waiting for the okay to continue.

"This is Lilah's fiancé, Killian," Brady tells the doctor as Nattie takes my hand in hers.

"The bullet caused a severe liver laceration. Too severe for non-surgical options to stop the bleeding. Once we got in, we found more damage than we hoped, but we were able to successfully repair the damage to the liver, though Lilah lost a lot of blood. I'm sorry, but we weren't able to save the baby."

"What?" I whisper as my knees threaten to give out.

Nattie grips me tighter, and my parents, who were trying to give us a false semblance of privacy, move to my other side.

"Lilah was in the very early stages of pregnancy. There was nothing we could do," the doctor tells us, and my entire vision narrows down to a pin dot on the wall.

"Can I see her? Is she awake?" I ask before her parents can speak, and tears stream down my face. I don't care that I'm in a waiting room full of people. I don't care that her mom and dad want to see her too. I don't care what my sister said. Lilah *is* everything. She's my everything.

"She's in recovery now. We're going to keep her there for a few hours. I'm sorry, but only one person is allowed back." He looks at Nattie, but Nattie looks at me with exhausted, tear-stained eyes.

"It should be you, Killian. She'll want to see you when she wakes up." She wraps her arms around my waist and squeezes. "But you tell our girl that her daddy and I are right here, and we can't wait to see her, okay?"

I nod with a heavy head and an even heavier heart.

"Take me to Lilah."

"She looks so pale," I say to the doctor, who follows me into the private recovery room.

"She's lost a lot of blood, but she's a fighter," he tells me, like I need a stranger to tell me this woman is a fighter. She's been a fighter her whole damn life.

"She saved me," I murmur, so fucking mad at her for that.

"I'm sorry we were unable to save the baby. But there was no permanent damage that would indicate any issues with her carrying to term in the future once Lilah has recovered."

The future . . .

This morning my future was set.

I was marrying the woman I've loved my whole fucking life, and now, I'm staring at her, knowing when she wakes up, I'm going to have to tell her we lost our baby.

I pull a chair next to her bed and sit down. "Can I touch her?"

"Yes. Hold her hand. Talk to her. Let her hear your voice. Studies show it helps." He checks something on one of the machines she's attached to, then moves toward the door. "A nurse will be in shortly to check on her again, and I'll be by again later. We normally wouldn't let you stay for longer than an hour, but no one will be asking you to leave, Mr. St. James."

"Thank you, Doctor. Thank you for everything," I tell him as I pick up Lilah's hand.

She's still cold, and I hate it.

She should be warm and smiling and full of life.

I should be the one in this bed.

I press my lips to her hands. "Wake up, princess. Show me those beautiful eyes. Yell at me for calling you princess, even though you really love the nickname." I drop my head to our hands. "I can't do this without you, Lilah. I need you. Please don't fucking leave me again."

Killian

Chapter 28

"Here, I brought you coffee." Maverick hands me the cup and stares at Lilah lying in the bed, a pink blanket her mom brought from home tucked around her. "She's still so damn pale."

"She's got more color today than yesterday." Barely, but it's there, and that's something.

At least that's what I keep telling myself.

"Rosie keeps asking if she can come see Tink. She's breaking my heart," he murmurs and takes Lilah's hand in his. "Mom's dog just had another litter of puppies. Rosie keeps asking if she can have one, and she told Mimi last night that she thinks Tink would want one too." I can't tell if he's telling me or Lilah until he bends down and whispers something into Lilah's ear and smiles.

"You need anything, Killer?"

"I need her to wake up," I tell him, like a robot. I feel nothing. Like I've shut down.

I look at the clock above the door.

It's been two days.

Mav looks away, like it's too much. "Did the doc say anything?"

I nod and put the coffee down, so I can pick her hand back up. "She'll wake up when she's ready."

"*B*rother, when was the last time you showered?" Noah asks as he squeezes my shoulder, and I sit up.

"Guess I fell asleep." I stand and stretch. "Is your mom okay? She was pretty upset when she left last night."

"She's not doing great. Asher said she hasn't slept in days. But at least she's showered." He drops a bag on my lap. "Brynn asked me to give this to you. I think it's clothes and shampoo. Go shower. And before you say you're not leaving, use the shower here. I won't leave her alone."

"No."

"Killian—"

"You don't get it. I can't leave her. She was in bed. She was safe and warm and happy, and she left to get me fucking pancakes. When I fell asleep, she was sleeping in my arms, and the next time I saw her, she was bleeding the fuck out. It's been four fucking days, and I can't do anything to help her. They can't tell us when she'll wake up, and the last thing I saw her do was take a bullet for me." I drag my fingers through my hair and get a whiff of myself. *Fuck.* I do need a damn shower.

"It wasn't supposed to be her. I was supposed to take the bullet. Not her. I was supposed to protect her. I was supposed to protect them both." *Fuck, I can't—* I grab the bag from the chair and point it at Noah with emotion clogging my throat. "Five minutes. Don't move from her side. I don't care who comes in here. Got it?"

Noah nods and wipes his eyes. "Don't forget the deodorant."

"Asshole."

"*K*illian, honey . . ." Nattie Ryan pulls up a chair next to me and places her hand over mine, so we're both holding Lilah's hand. "Noah said he got you to shower earlier. Is there any chance I can get you to eat something? I picked up some soup from The Busy Bee."

"I'm okay, thanks."

Brady watches us from the door. Standing guard over his daughter and wife.

Strong enough to let me be the man sitting next to Lilah, even though I know he's got to wish it was him holding her hand.

"She's going to wake up," Nattie chants, pushing her thoughts out into the universe. "She has to. Our girl has too much to live for not to wake up."

"She's your daughter, sweetheart. She's never been on time for anything in her life." Brady moves behind Nattie and kisses the top of her head, then places a hand on my back. "I hope you're prepared for a lifetime of living at her whim."

"I don't care what she does, so long as she gives me a lifetime."

I crack open my eyes and rub my face when something tickles my cheek.

"Hey, sleepyhead," her beautiful soft voice whispers, and I lift my head from her bed. "Lilah . . . ? Oh God, baby. You're awake. I'm not dreaming?" I press my lips to her forehead. "We've got to call the nurse."

"Wait," her voice cracks. "What happened?"

She runs her fingers through my hair, and I could cry, I'm so goddamn happy to feel that simple touch.

I pull back, so I can look down at her face. "What do you remember?"

"I remember . . . Zoe." Her eyes scan my face before they close. "I came back from The Busy Bee, and Zoe was at the house."

Her beautiful blue eyes pop back, confusion written in every line on her face.

"What else?" I ask, not wanting her to have to relive that hell but knowing she's better off hearing it from me than the police, who are going to want to question her in a few hours, once they know she's awake.

Tear-filled, those eyes grow wide with fear that I wish I could take away. "She had a gun . . . Oh my God, Killian. Did she shoot you? Are you okay?"

I kiss away the tears streaming down her cheeks. "I'm fine, baby. But you weren't. She shot you. The bullet hit your liver. They rushed you into surgery, but you're going to be fine," I promise her, vowing it from the depths of my fucking soul. I press my lips to her forehead. "You're going to be fine."

"I remember thinking she was going to shoot you. I had to stop her."

Her voice takes on a hysterical tone, and I push out of the chair that's been my bed for the last four days and climb into bed with her. "Never again, Lilah. You never step in front of anyone or anything for me. You let me protect you. Not the other way around."

"I'm sorry. I couldn't let her hurt you. I don't even know what she was doing there. She was talking about loving me and protecting me. It was—she sounded like you."

I run my hand over her hair and kiss her head. "She shot you, Lilah, because you stepped between her and me, and then Xander shot her. When the police searched her house, they gathered so much evidence. She was obsessed with you. She'd been obsessed with you for years. She had scrapbooks and pictures and pieces of your costumes. She had plans for the bomb they found in your dressing room on her computer and a panic room built into her basement with enough tranquilizers stored there to put down a whole fucking football team. They found forged passports that never would have passed security checks for you and her."

Lilah gasps, and the sound destroys me.

"How did we not know?"

I hold her tighter to me. "She was delusional, princess. They think in her mind, you two were in love. Us getting engaged sent her into a rage."

"It was her? The bomber? The stalker? It was her?" Her voice trembles and guts me.

"Yeah, it was her." I tuck Lilah's head against my chest and press my face to her hair. "According to a journal they found, the bomb was supposed to take out enough people that the tour would be canceled, and you'd be sent home to her. She thought that would be her chance to get you away and have you to herself."

"How long have I been out?" she whispers.

I kiss her again, so fucking scared of the things I still have to tell her. "You've been out for four days, baby. But you're going to be okay. The tour is going to have to be canceled though. Your recovery is going to take at least six months."

"What aren't you telling me?" The words are soft and slow and scared, and I know this is going to be one of those moments in my life I'll never forget, and I'll always hate myself for it.

I wait as long as I can, trying to force down the emotion building in my throat as I stare into her frightened eyes.

Wishing I could shield her from this pain.

But knowing I can't.

I suck in a deep breath, but it doesn't help.

Nothing will.

"Lilah . . . you were pregnant."

It's the first time I've said the words since the doctor told us.

And it guts me all over again.

I didn't save them.

Either of them.

"I'm so fucking sorry I couldn't save you."

"What?" she asks as a sob catches in her throat. "I wasn't pregnant. I would have known."

"It was early. There was too much damage. Too much blood." I choke on the words and wrap both arms around Lilah as she shakes.

"We lost our baby? I never even knew I was pregnant, and she took that from us?" she cries, and my heart breaks all over again.

"I'm so sorry, baby." I hold her, murmuring the words over and over again while she soaks my shirt with her tears.

I'm not sure how much time passes before she has no more tears to shed.

"You have nothing to be sorry for, Killian. None of this is your fault. It's not mine either. We didn't do this. A crazy woman did." Her breathing stutters, and she presses a hand to my heart. "Will we be able to have more kids?"

The question is barely above a whisper of a breath into the dark hospital room, she utters it so quietly.

"The doctor said there shouldn't be any issue when you're ready," I tell her with my lips pressed against her temple. "I love you so much, Lilah. I swear to God, if I had lost you, they would have been burying me beside you. I don't want to live in a world you're not in, princess."

Her breathing slows, and long minutes later, she kisses my cheek. "Hey, champ . . ." Her voice is soft and quiet but not broken. She's here and she's breathing and she's mine. We can deal with everything else together. "I don't really hate that nickname. I kinda love the way you say it."

"I will love you forever, Lilah. From my first breath until my last. In every life," I whisper against her lips.

"From my first breath until my last . . . That's a great lyric," she says as she clutches my shirt. "In every life. In every way."

"Always us . . ." I swear to God, I take my first deep, full breath in days.

"Forever."

Forever.

The best part of my day is you. Always you. Forever you.

—Killian's Secret Thoughts

"Does Mav seem more pissed than normal?" Lilah asks from where she's sitting in my lap in front of the bonfire on our private stretch of beach. We decided to forgo traditional bachelor and bachelorette parties for a beach party with our closest friends instead.

In our world, it's perfect. Low-key. Private. And steps away from the houses we're all crashing in tonight and tomorrow before our wedding on Saturday.

"He prefers broody." I smile and bury my face in her neck the way I'm going to bury my face in her lace-covered pussy later tonight.

"Who prefers broody?" Jamie asks as he drops down into the Adirondack chair next to us. "Fuck . . . you guys aren't working on nicknames for Killian's dick, are you?"

"Dude—" I look for something to throw at him and come up empty. "She doesn't call my dick broody, you asshole."

Lilah giggles and traces my earlobe with her tongue. "I

can if you want me to," she whispers, and I slide my hand up under her short white dress and dig my fingers into her ass.

Fuck, I love this woman.

"Go fuck in the outdoor shower like the rest of the family," Dillan laughs as she stands in front of the fire with a wine glass in her hand. "Maybe not Mom and Dad's though. I'm pretty sure one of our cousins is in there with one of Killian's cousins."

"What? Who? And with who?" Lilah asks as she scrambles off my lap and takes Dillan's hand excitedly.

"I'm not sure. It's just a hunch." Dillan and Lilah look like the spitting image of their mother, standing next to each other, and I get a flash of fear for my future. *Boys*. When we have kids one day, they need to be boys, so I don't kill every dumb punk that comes near my daughters.

Fuck. I'm going to jail.

"Oh my God," Lilah squeals, a little tipsy from her drink. The first she's had since the shooting four months ago. "Come with me." She tugs Dillan. "Now I need to know."

Lilah drags Dillan behind her out of my sight, and I stand from my chair and watch them go, until they disappear behind Nattie and Brady's gate.

"She's only right there, Killer," Noah tells me from the chair next to mine, while he strums Baby as I wait and watch.

"Yeah, man. I know. Still doesn't make it easier though," I admit, with my whole damn chest feeling tight. Because while I know I have to let Lilah live her life and let her out of my sight, it's fucking hard to do. Visions of that morning still plague my dreams. A living, breathing, nightmare we both deal with every day. The media frenzy after what happened has forced a level of security my girl will never be okay with, but she no longer fights it.

I push away the fucked up thoughts and turn back to

Noah. "She said the meeting with the lawyers earlier went well."

He holds his hand over the guitar strings, stopping the music and grins. "Yeah, it fucking did. We signed the contracts. Blue Bell Records is in business, and Lilah St. James is the first act we signed."

I hear Lilah's laughter and catch her and Dillan stumbling away from their parents' yard.

Fuck. I can't wait for her to be my wife.

Wait—what?

"Lilah what?" I ask, because she's not taking my name.

Not professionally.

"Fuck." Noah looks from his sisters back to me. "You didn't hear anything."

He swings Baby over his back and heads for the house. "Nothing, St. James. You didn't hear a thing."

"Umm . . . what the hell is Noah bitching about?" Dillan asks as she and Lilah laugh, stumbling over the dunes, clinging to each other. Both a little off-balance.

"Lilah . . ." I lift her up as she steps in to me and then sit us both back down in the chair. "What's this I hear about Blue Bell Records signing its first act?"

Her cheeks heat, and she rolls her eyes. "Noah," she yells. "You little bitch."

She pulls her knees up to my chest and tucks herself against me. "I liked it better when he was keeping things from everyone."

"No, you didn't," I laugh and take a pull of my beer. "So you want to tell me what he's talking about, princess?"

"Yeah, *princess*? How about you speak loud enough for the crowd?" Maverick teases, dryly as he stops on the other side of the fire.

"Oh, *princess* . . ." Jamie taunts, and she flips them both the

241

finger while Dillan raises her glass of wine to them both. Always defending her sister.

"Fine." She looks up at all the guys and Dillan and shakes her head. "I told you he'd find out."

"I told you, you should make him fuck it out of you." Dillan hiccups and finishes her wine. "My way would have been way more fun than this." She shrugs and smiles.

"I see nothing wrong with that," I murmur against Lilah's hair.

"Fine," Lilah huffs. "You already knew I was taking your name Saturday. But I wanted to surprise you and tell you that Blue Bell Records signed our first act today . . . me."

"Sounds like nepotism to me," Maverick heckles.

"Fuck off, Mav. You play for your mommy's team," my girl bites back, pretty as can be.

"Focus, princess. You signed yourself to the label you own, and . . . ?" I prompt her.

"Co-own with your mother. King Corp. owns 49 percent."

They do.

Lilah owns the other 51 percent.

"And . . ." I push.

"And I decided that when it's announced next week, I wanted it announced that Lilah St. James is joining Blue Bell Records. Lilah Ryan was before I married you, and I can't fucking wait to marry you, champ."

"Have I ever told you how sexy it is when you curse, baby?" I brush my lips over hers, my cock rock hard under her sweet little ass.

"Oh, eww," Dillan groans. "I think I just threw up in my mouth a little."

"Is that what you're into?" Maddox asks as he slings an arm over her shoulder.

"Wouldn't you like to find out?" she volleys back.

"I'd totally volunteer for that mission," Rome announces over his beer, and it's Lilah's turn to groan. "I'm a good man to have on the job, little Ryan. Focused. Determined."

"Dream on, psycho," Dillan laughs.

"Hey, guys," Lilah calls out to no one and everyone all at once. "I love you guys."

"And . . . that's enough." I stand with her in my arms. "I'm the only one that gets your I love you's, baby."

"Now I'm gonna puke," Jamie jokes, and I mouth *fuck off* as I walk away with my girl in my arms and my friends busting my balls about being whipped.

They can all fuck off because if they had what I have, they'd be happily whipped too.

And two nights later, when Noah lifts the microphone to his face during our reception, I realize they all know it too.

"The first time I knew Killian loved Lilah, we were eight years old. We'd just gotten out of the pool at our parents' house, and Lilah was crying with a dead butterfly in her hand. Side note—I still think she squeezed it to death. But either way, she was heartbroken. Big, fat, crocodile tears flooded her face, and while Jamie, Maverick, and I all laughed, Killian patted her back, like he was scared if he touched her he'd get cooties, and then he helped her bury it in a shoe box. And Lilah made him dig that hole deep, so our dog couldn't dig it up and eat it. She was really worried about that." Noah lifts his beer in the air and smiles at us, and Lilah wipes at her eyes.

"We all knew we'd be sitting at your wedding one day. And I'm especially grateful to get to be one of both the bride and groom's three best men. Not exactly traditional, but nothing you two ever did followed any kind of traditional path."

She rests her head on my shoulder and sighs the prettiest

sound, and I can't help but cherish every minute. So completely aware of how lucky we are to be here.

"I'd like you all to raise your glasses and join me in a toast." Noah turns to us and winks. "To the new Mr. and Mrs. St. James. There's never been another couple as destined to be together as you. I love you guys."

"He's right, you know." I cup her face in my hands. "I've loved you my whole life."

I wipe her tear with my thumb, and she smiles. "And I'll love you for the rest of mine."

The End
Want more Lilah & Killian?
Download their extended epilogue!

Download the extended epilogue here

The Philly Press

KROYDON KRONICLES

NOT READY TO SAY GOODBYE YET?

Are you ready to see which Kroydon Hills resident falls next?

There's plenty of secrets they've been keeping from you, and you're not going to believe what they are.

Make sure to preorder *Teasing*, book 5 in *Red Lips & White Lies*, to see what secrets and who has been keeping them...

Preorder Teasing Now

#KroydonKronicles #Teasing

If you haven't read the first book in the Kings Of Kroydon Hills series, you can start with *All In* today!

Read All In for FREE on KU

ACKNOWLEDGMENTS

Thank you so much to my family for all your support. My husband and children are my world, and my time with them often gets sacrificed for my time with these characters.

Thank you to my amazing team. I cannot imagine doing this without each and every one of you. Dena, Callie, Jen, Tammy, Hannah, Morgan, Valentine, Val, Julie and Shannon - I have no words big enough to show my appreciation. And to my Happy Hunting girlies, thanks for cheering me on. Killian & Lilah are better because of you.

And to my incredible momager, Bri. One more down and an infinite number of books still to go. Thank you for managing my business and my life.

As always, my biggest thanks goes to you, the reader, for taking a chance on Killian & Lilah, and this fictional town I love so much. I hope you enjoyed reading *Captivating* as much as I've enjoyed writing it.

ABOUT THE AUTHOR

Bella Matthews is a *USA Today* & #1 Amazon Bestselling author. She is married to her very own Alpha Male and raising three little ones. You can typically find her running from one sporting event to another. When she is home, she is usually hiding in her home office with the only other female in her house, her rescue dog Tinker Bell by her side. She likes to write swoon-worthy heroes and sassy, smart heroines. Sarcasm is her love language and big family dynamics are her favorite thing to add to each story.

Stay Connected
Amazon Author Page: https://amzn.to/2UWU7Xs
Facebook Page: https://www.facebook.com/Bella.
Matthews.Author
Reader Group: https://www.facebook.com/groups/
bellamatthewsgamechangers
Instagram: https://www.instagram.com/bellamatthews.
author/
Bookbub: https://bit.ly/BMBookbub
Goodreads: https://bit.ly/BMGoodreads
TikTok: http://tiktok.com/@bellamatthewsauthor
Newsletter: https://bit.ly/BMNLsingups
Patreon: https://www.patreon.com/BellaMatthews

ALSO BY BELLA MATTHEWS

Kings of Kroydon Hills

All In

More Than A Game

Always Earned, Never Given

Under Pressure

Restless Kings

Rise of the King

Broken King

Fallen King

The Risks We Take Duet

Worth The Risk

Worth The Fight

Defiant Kings

Caged

Shaken

Iced

Overruled

Haven

Playing To Win

The Keeper

The Wildcat

The Knockout

The Sweet Spot

Red Lips & White Lies

Tempting

Redeeming

Enticing

Captivating

Teasing

Breathtaking

Love & Legacy

TBA - coming 2025

TBA - coming 2025

CHECK OUT BELLA'S WEBSITE

Scan the QR code or go to http://authorbellamatthews.com
to stay up to date with all things Bella Matthews

Made in United States
Orlando, FL
18 February 2025

58672385R00163